He Could Wait.

Austin needed Iris to get used to him, to be comfortable with him. Then they could talk. He was older than she, and more worldly.

Worldly? She'd had *three* husbands!

Well, they'd all been kids. And she hadn't had any of them long enough to really be tested. She needed permanence and maturity.

She needed...him.

He looked over at Iris. Her cold little hand was warming in his big hot hand. Hers was lax and...trusting? Did she trust him?

Would she ever trust him enough to love him?

Dear Reader,

Spring is in the air—and all thoughts turn toward love. With six provocative romances from Silhouette Desire, you too can enjoy a season of new beginnings...and happy endings!

Our March MAN OF THE MONTH is Lass Small's *The Best Husband in Texas*. This sexy rancher is determined to win over the beautiful widow he's loved for years! Next, Joan Elliott Pickart returns with a wonderful love story—*Just My Joe*. Watch sparks fly between handsome, wealthy Joe Dillon and the woman he loves.

Don't miss Beverly Barton's new miniseries, 3 BABIES FOR 3 BROTHERS, which begins with *His Secret Child*. The town golden boy is reunited with a former flame—and their child. Popular Anne Marie Winston offers the third title in her BUTLER COUNTY BRIDES series, as a sexy heroine forms a partnership with her lost love in *The Bride Means Business*. Then an expectant mom matches wits with a brooding rancher in Carol Grace's *Expecting*.... And Virginia Dove debuts explosively with *The Bridal Promise*, when star-crossed lovers marry for convenience.

This spring, please write and tell us why you read Silhouette Desire books. As part of our 20th anniversary celebration in the year 2000, we'd like to publish some of this fan mail in the books—so drop us a line, tell us how long you've been reading Desire books and what you love about the series. And enjoy our March titles!

Regards,

Joan Marlow Golan
Senior Editor, Silhouette Desire

Please address questions and book requests to:
Silhouette Reader Service
U.S.: 3010 Walden Ave., P.O. Box 1325, Buffalo, NY 14269
Canadian: P.O. Box 609, Fort Erie, Ont. L2A 5X3

LASS SMALL
THE BEST HUSBAND IN TEXAS

SILHOUETTE *Desire*

Published by Silhouette Books

America's Publisher of Contemporary Romance

SILHOUETTE BOOKS

ISBN 0-373-76201-1

THE BEST HUSBAND IN TEXAS

This edition published by arrangement with Harlequin Books S.A.

® and TM are trademarks of Harlequin Books S.A., used under license. Trademarks indicated with ® are registered in the United States Patent and Trademark Office, the Canadian Trade Marks Office and in other countries.

Printed in U.S.A.

Books by Lass Small

Tangled Web #241
To Meet Again #322
Stolen Day #341
Possibles #356
Intrusive Man #373
To Love Again #397
Blindman's Bluff #413
Goldilocks and the Behr #437
Hide and Seek #453
Red Rover #491
Odd Man Out #505
Tagged #534
Contact #548
Wrong Address, Right Place #569
Not Easy #578
The Loner #594
Four Dollars and Fifty-One Cents #613
No Trespassing Allowed #638
The Molly Q #655
† *'Twas the Night* #684
Dominic #697
†*A Restless Man* #731
†*Two Halves* #743
†*Beware of Widows* #755
A Disruptive Influence #775
†*Balanced* #800
†*Tweed* #817
†*A New Year* #830
†*I'm Gonna Get You* #848
†*Salty and Felicia* #860
†*Lemon* #879
†*An Obsolete Man* #895
A Nuisance #901
Impulse #926
Whatever Comes #963
My House or Yours? #974
A Stranger in Texas #994
The Texas Blue Norther #1027
The Coffeepot Inn #1045
Chancy's Cowboy #1064
How To Win (Back) a Wife #1107
‡*Taken by a Texan* #1137
‡*The Hard-To-Tame Texan* #1148
‡*The Lone Texan* #1165
The Best Husband in Texas #1201

Silhouette Romance

An Irritating Man #444
Snow Bird #521

Silhouette Yours Truly

Not Looking for a Texas Man
*The Case of the Lady in
  Apartment 308*

Silhouette Books

Silhouette Christmas Stories 1989
"Voice of the Turtles"
Silhouette Spring Fancy 1993
"Chance Encounter"

*Lambert Series
†Fabulous Brown Brothers
‡ The Keepers of Texas

LASS SMALL

finds living on this planet at this time a fascinating experience. People are amazing. She thinks that to be a teller of tales of people, places and things is absolutely marvelous.

To Debra Robertson

One

At the age of nineteen, Iris Smith Osburn lost her first husband to Desert Storm. A U.S. tank ran over Jake's foxhole. Since the tank was one of ours, the government—with some earnest coaxing in court—paid up.

There in San Antonio, TEXAS, the grieving Iris voluntarily split the award with her late husband's hostile family. They thought she was selfish, but sourly they took the lawyer-settled half of the money. The attorney's fees came from her half.

Iris Smith Osburn Dallas's second husband was her first husband's best friend. He was a fine man, and like her first husband, he was very gentle and kind. Tom died of some strange Gulf disease that's still being studied. He, too, had been in Desert Storm and there was government insurance. He had no family who wanted to share.

Her third husband was a friend to the second. Peter Alden was charming. Iris was reluctant to try marriage again, but Peter was adamant, and he convinced her to become his wife. While a spectator at a rodeo, he was trampled by a nasty bull that had gotten loose between the fences. Peter's death had been quick. It had been a shock that had shaken Iris to the core.

The female mourners who were at Peter Alden's funeral whispered that, each time, Iris's grief had been quite practiced. They whispered that with her hands over her face that way, she was probably looking through her fingers to see who would be her next?

Iris Smith Osburn Dallas Alden not only was awarded the life insurance of her third husband, but her brother-in-law was an attorney. He proved the rodeo proprietors were responsible. He gently refused his fee.

Iris offered Peter's family half of the compensation awarded by the Court's judgment. The family declined. They discouraged their lawyer son's attentions to the blond, blue-eyed Iris. Obviously, she was dangerous to men.

She moved back home to Fuquay, about eighty miles north and west of San Antonio near Kerrville. Iris was, by then, twenty-four years old and three times a widow. All of her marriages had been brief. She felt she was a scourge and knew she would never marry again.

It was February of that year when Iris was welcomed back among her relatives and friends with varying reactions. Her extended family was mostly compassionate. There were those who considered her a threat. There was just something about a young, good-looking, grieving widow that lured men. Then, too, she was financially well-off...another very strong lure to most men.

Eldest of the children in her family, it was very strange for Iris to be back in Fuquay, TEXAS, to live at home again. But she could not deal with curiosity. She needed her family's protection.

The house was very familiar because it hadn't changed much over the years. It was filled with family hand-me-down furniture and hand-crocheted curtains. Even to strangers, it was a comfortable house.

Iris knew that her own room had not been used because there were so many unoccupied rooms. She could go into her old room, close the door and be alone. The house was silent. It felt as if it was frozen in time. Just about the way Iris was. Both were on hold. Waiting? For what?

Iris looked with dead eyes at the pictures still on her bulletin board. Who was that long-ago child who'd saved those curled pictures? Who was that laughing woman? She'd had a good laugh, which hadn't been heard in some time.

She could not recall when she had last laughed. About what?

On that board, there were no pictures of any of her husbands. It was as if her life had stopped when she'd left this silent, still house. And she'd come back to it as a ghost.

Iris opened one of the room's windows to TEXAS's February-fresh mildness. They were due a norther. Maybe if she opened all the windows, the house would be refreshed and shake itself back to life?

What about her? Could she then begin to breathe and again be the woman who had left here to move to San Antonio to go to Incarnate Word College? That was…several lifetimes ago.

No.

She could not go back in time. But she couldn't find the motivation to get herself to go forward. She was lost. She would never marry again. It was too awful to have a partner who failed in the sworn commitment of "from this day forward." Why had she buried three such good young men?

At twenty-four, she was older now than either of her first two husbands. Iris and her husbands' families would never know what sort of men they would have become, what careers they would have chosen or what their children could have been.

Her tears welled.

She knew she would never again marry. She could not stand to be another man's widow. She was a curse. The realization, the clarity of their unfulfilled lives had caught up with her and overwhelmed her to the point that she didn't know how to cope. Therefore she withdrew. She was in a capsule of her own making. In there she was alone, and it was silent.

With chidings and scoldings, people tried to drag her out. She endured. But she would withdraw as soon as she could manage it in a careful, subtle way.

Her mother watched her. Her daddy was impatient with her and scolded...her mother. But her mother said, "Leave her be for a while. This has been the straw." She was referring to the straw piled on the straw that finally broke the camel's back.

How could her mother realize so exactly the burden of grief Iris carried?

Her sisters' reactions were split between compassion and irritation. They would scold her and try to bring her out of her shell. They weren't successful.

Despite his busy life, her young brother would sit with her in silence, demanding nothing of her. He was there. He fixed a car part. He wrote a letter. He watched TV. He studied. He was there for her.

She really didn't notice.

Their friends in Fuquay were very kind and thoughtful of Iris. They were also nosy, but they were reasonably subtle about it. Just that Iris had had *three* husbands was enough to irritate any number of her unmarried female friends.

Iris's high school chum Marla's response was simple. She had twins and she'd hand one of them to Iris—to distract her.

Holding the wiggly baby only made Iris think that none of her three husbands had left her a part of him. "We got time," they each had said. They'd be logical. "What's the rush?" "Let's spend this time with it being just us."

And it was. Except that, now, she was alone. Alone in the midst of her ordinary, busy family. So alone was Iris in her silence, she could hear the air pop. And she watched the clock. That baffled everyone. If she couldn't see her watch or the clock, she asked, "What time is it?"

They'd inquire with puzzled interest, "You going somewheres?"

Her glance would come to theirs and she'd say, "No."

"You waiting for a program on TV?"

"No."

She confused them.

She wanted time to get on past. She had nothing to do that was important enough to help with it. So she depended on a clock to get it done...to get the time past.

Their neighbor at the ranch down the road, Austin Farrell, wanted to be Iris's fourth husband. He'd been named for Stephen F. Austin who had brought settlers to TEXAS long, long ago. Well, in TEXAS history, it was a long time. Actually it wasn't yet two hundred years.

Austin Farrell was a heel-dug, obstinate, good man almost thirty. He was about six feet tall and had land that was productive; and it was all paid for, even the taxes. His eyes were a gray that was strangely blue, and his face was tanned under his Stetson. He wanted Iris. He was a TEXAN. He'd get her.

However, Iris had come to feel like the poisonous Lucrezia Borgia, duchess of Ferrara. That title was shockingly close to Austin's last name. The Duchess had lived in Italy from 1480-1519. In that time, Lucrezia had dispatched any number of lovers.

Iris Smith Osburn Dallas Alden felt similarly deadly. However, she hadn't even needed the poison. She herself was the curse. And she didn't want another dead husband.

Not knowing her mother was a party to Austin's plans, Iris declined his invitation to go to a play when he arrived at the house one day to visit.

He said, "The play has a funny story, and it'll make you laugh."

The idea of laughing at *anything* was so incredible that Iris gave Austin a glance to see if he was serious.

He was.

So Iris replied bitterly, "I'm the TEXAS version of Lucrezia Borgia. Look what I've done to three good husbands."

Although his eyes squinted just a little bit in compassion, Austin was gently, rather aloofly chiding. "I just asked if you'd like to go with me over to San Antone to the play at the Majestic Theatre. I haven't yet asked to marry you."

Iris looked at Austin suspiciously.

He smiled a little and suggested, "Who would you like along as chaperone?"

Iris was distracted. But her mother was leaning

in the doorway, listening, and she told Iris, "You really ought to go to the play." Edwina Smith was a smart woman. She understood Iris's baffled reaction, and she had offered Iris an opinion.

Iris considered Austin. He'd told her to pick a chaperone. She mentally shuffled through her acquaintances. She chose Violet who was too shy to flirt. This would be good practice for her friend Violet.

Iris told Austin, "Violet. And teach her to flirt. Help her."

Austin's heart faltered and he glanced over at Edwina Smith for courage. Iris's mother smiled the tiniest bit. But it was a sad smile.

Austin became staunch. He'd explain the circumstances to Violet and help her to meet any male she might cotton to.

Iris did go to the play. They doubled. Austin and his friend, Bud, escorted the two...flowers, Iris and Violet. That they were so named was cause for drollness. The women had grown up together and were used to it.

To Austin's displeasure, Bud made a move for *Iris!*

Austin growled, "It's to Violet that you're *supposed* to be paying attention. You leave Iris alone."

Bud smiled.

Austin spent the first part of the evening switching Iris to his other side and blocking Bud's advances. Austin told Bud that old hack, "You've got great teeth."

Bud smiled toothily.

And gently Austin added, "I'd hate for anything to happen to them."

The twenty-six-year-old Bud's eyes narrowed as he considered how much of a threat a mature man, who was almost thirty, would be.

Austin smiled rather widely.

Bud noted the chipped tooth in Austin's smile and remembered how he'd gotten it. He happened to notice all the scars on Austin's bare, sunbrowned knuckles, and he came to the conclusion that it wasn't worth the effort to tangle with such a man.

The play was a road show of *You Can't Take it with You.* And no matter how many times the cast had performed it, they made it appear fresh.

The theme of *You Can't Take it with You* was to live your life. A good comment. It was the reason Austin had taken Iris to see it. Only twenty-four years old, she still had a long life ahead of her. She shouldn't waste it. And while she didn't yet realize it, she had Austin to consider.

Watching the play, Iris only understood that her husbands hadn't had the chance to live out their lives. Instead of stimulating her, the play only made her excruciatingly aware of how young her husbands had been when they died. How much they'd missed. How short were their lives. How they'd been…cheated. She grieved for them.

It hadn't occurred to Austin that Iris would take such a route of thinking. Amid the laughter of the audience, he uneasily monitored her withdrawn silence.

He wondered, for which one did she grieve?

How could he ask?

When the play was over, they moved with the cheerful crowd to leave the preserved theatre, and they walked to the car over by Travis Park Square. Bud drove. He watched the pair in the back seat in the rearview mirror.

They sat apart.

Each looked out a different side window.

In the back seat, in a low voice, Austin asked Iris, "You okay?"

She slowly blinked, then turned her head to look at him. He had to repeat his question. Then she nodded.

Austin was struck by that. How unlike a woman to neglect an opportunity to expound on such a question. To think of all the nothing replies she could have given him. She could have said, As compared to what? Or, Under what condition? Or even just, Why? Or she could explain to him why she was in such doldrums. He would like to know.

Dead in the water, she was.

Austin again looked at Iris. He moved his mouth in thought. Dead in the water described Iris very well. No response. No animation. No flirting. No laughter.

She moved, but it wasn't animation. It was by rote in response to the need to shift or walk or eat. With her, it wasn't ever choice. It was response. Austin wondered, was there enough life left in that luscious body? How could he reach in to rouse her enough to see *him* as a man she was interested in. One she could want.

She sat looking out the car window and was silent. He considered that she, too, was dead. Just about as dead as those three ex-husbands of hers. What good was her life now? She was as removed from life as if she now actually shared their graves.

So then Austin wondered which of the three graves she'd choose to share?

Austin was appalled to find he would wish to be one of the three with that claim on her. Each of those dead men had loved her enough to marry her. To be with her. To listen to her. They'd made love with her. Had she ever laughed with them?

Compassion for the three men licked through Austin, but he didn't back off. Instead, he took

Iris's hand and held it in his. Their hands were linked between them, her cold little hand lying in his big hot one on the back seat as they sat apart.

His hand holding hers was very comforting to the freshly stirred grief that her conscience had awakened in Iris.

Would she ever be free of the guilt she suffered because her husbands were all dead, and she was still alive? All three had been especially good men.

Austin moved his hand as his warm, briefly tightening fingers assured her he was there.

He had the good, square, warm, rough hand of a man who worked physically. It was emotional for Iris to be given that comfort, right then. Her eyes teared.

Austin saw her tears in the glow of the passing streetlamps. Tears? Why…tears? He considered her particular situation and the teaching of the play.

Austin knew that Iris had understood the play, but instead of looking ahead to life, he realized that she was looking back at her abandonment. Was she alone? She could hardly be alone in her noisy, busy family. *If* she noticed who all was actually there with her.

Was she thinking of the loss of her husbands? The waste of their lives. How could anyone tell her that what had happened, had happened, and it was all past?

The play gave him the courage to open a discussion. "It was a good play."

After a pause, she replied, "Yes."

"Live for the day."

She did not respond. But she didn't move her cold little hand from the shelter of his hot one.

Austin wasn't sure if he could say anything else. It might be too emotional for her. It was the first time they'd been out together—with Bud and Violet, of course—and this might not be the time to start her talking.

He could wait. He needed her to get used to him, to be comfortable with him. Then they could talk. He was older than she, and he was more worldly.

Worldly? She'd had *three* husbands!

Well, they'd all been kids. They'd been young and raw. And she hadn't had any of them long enough to really be tested. She needed permanence and maturity.

She needed...him.

He again looked over at her. Her cold little hand was warming in his big hot hand. Hers was lax and...trustful? Did she trust him? She was looking at the passing suburbs of San Antonio as they drove through town toward the highway that went to Fuquay.

In the front seat, Bud was regaling Violet with all the old jokes that had obviously been stacked up inside him. Violet never once said, "Not that old one." She either had a compassionate heart or no one had ever subjected her to all those old, stale jokes. Actually—and it was a surprise—Bud was a pretty good jokester. His timing was good. And here and there even Austin had to smile.

Iris did not. She simply gazed out the car window and was silent.

Austin just sat holding her hand and he, too, was silent.

It was rather late when Iris got home. Her mother heard Iris's light step on the porch followed more slowly by the reverberation of Austin's shoes on the porch.

The screen opened and closed almost immediately. On the porch the male steps were silent. Then Austin turned slowly and finally went off down the steps as he left.

When Iris went upstairs to her room in her parents' house, her mind was not in charge. It was off somewhere. She moved by rote. She undressed and crawled into bed without brushing her teeth.

Emotionally exhausted, she slept. She dreamed of looking for her husbands. She searched for them. She was the only stranger in all the places she searched. But she couldn't contact them at all.

Where were they?

Her dead husbands were good, young men. Would they be together? Jake and Tom were friends, and Peter had known Tom. Would they have met? Would they have talked about her with each other? When she died, would they all greet her? Or would they be...in the beyond?

Iris wakened, and found her eyes wet with tears. She still grieved for those husbands.

Her life was over. How long would she have to wait to get past this life and find them again?

The play had chided the audience to use their lives while they had them. Ah, but what if the use was gone? What if there was no reason to go on?

She had married *three* men. None was now with her. And *none* had left her with a child. They had all left her...alone.

Iris went about the morning as usual. She was drained. She looked at the day with disinterested, cold eyes. It was just another day to get through.

At breakfast, as she sipped tea, Iris's mother came into the kitchen and said her usual, "Good morning, darling."

Iris asked, "Which am I?"

Her mother poured some tea into a cup before she replied, "The wounded one."

Iris considered that response. "Yeah. I suppose

that covers it. I have three deep slashes in my heart."

Tears in her eyes, her mother replied, "That describes it well."

"Austin took me to see *You Can't Take it with You* last night."

"Yes."

"Do you know the play?"

"Very well."

With her voice's rough shattering, Iris asked, "How can I find any reason to enjoy this life?"

It took a while for her mother to reply. "You can look at the day and the people who live in it. You can look forward instead of backward."

Her voice trembling with tears, Iris guessed, "I discard each one and forget them all?"

"No. You...release them...and let them go."

Her voice husky and bitter, Iris asked, "I tell them to just run along and get lost?"

And her mother replied gently, "You must let them go."

"They're in my mind!"

"You've trapped them there."

"No!" Iris got up and left the room with her breakfast almost untouched.

Not eating was one of Iris's problems. Not eating, and not caring what happened. She was afraid to be close to anyone, so she was gruff and distancing to all those around her. It was self-protection. She didn't want to love and lose anyone else.

Edwina wondered when the time would come that Iris would reach out? To whom? For what reason? What would it take for this fragile, wounded child of hers to see the world...and to be a part of it again?

Two

Iris came down the stairs in a soft, long, rumpled dress and her hair hadn't been brushed very well. She'd probably just clawed her fingers through her hair.

Without any greeting, Austin told her of his cow as Iris came down the last steps. "You remember Fanny? She has a new calf. Come see it." He didn't smile or coax. He gave her the unadorned option.

Iris questioned, "New?"

Austin agreed. "Joe just called in on the CB. The momma was licking the sack from her baby just before I got here. I really thought I'd get you back there in time for the birth."

Austin watched Iris. She just moved on past him slowly but she went on out the door. With a quiet glance at the riveted Edwina, the silent Austin followed the silent Iris.

Since Iris moved slowly, Austin got to the truck ahead of her and opened the door for her.

She just got up into the pickup and sat there with her hands clasped on her lap.

Austin hurried around the truck and got in real quick and started the motor. He was very aware that if Iris could get in that easily, she could get out just as quick.

He noted that her seat belt wasn't on her. But he couldn't stay there to correct it because she could change her mind, get out of the truck—and leave. So he drove carefully to the edge of Fuquay before he said, "Hey, our seat belts aren't on."

And he helped with hers… Ah, for his own arms to be given the job of protecting her body! His eyes squinched and his mouth opened a little bit so that he could breathe.

She made no move to help with the belt and didn't even watch him fix it. She just moved her arm and allowed herself to be safeguarded.

Only after she was secure did he buckle his own belt. She made no comment.

While his mind noted the weather, his neighbor's livestock and other vehicles on the road, he also noted every breath and move Iris made as she sat silently in the cab of his pickup.

Finally he said, "Violet and Bud had another date."

Iris made a sound in reply that meant only that she'd heard him.

He said, "Marla's twins have the croup."

He'd spent time that morning talking to Iris's friend Marla and getting the gossip so that he'd have something to say to such a silent woman. Even if she didn't reply or discuss each item, she would know the current gossip.

Thoughtfully, Austin looked over at Iris. And he wondered, would she?

She just turned her head to look out the car window and said nothing. Was her mind gone? Would her eyes ever see him? Why had she gone into the decline? Since she came home, it seemed to Austin that she just got worse.

If she didn't have all the money from her dead husbands, she'd have to get out and work. She'd have to have some contact with other people. Edwina said Iris prowled the dark house at night.

So Austin asked Iris, "Do you sleep during the day?"

"No."

Then why did she…prowl…at night?

The day was balmy and the fresh air came over the land from the Gulf and into the pickup.

Austin told his passenger, "Breathe that TEXAS air. It's good for your vitals."

Very softly, she replied, "*I* can breathe." None of her dead husbands could.

Austin blinked. He knew she could breathe. What did she mean? He frowned at the road, wondering if he should ask. But he bit his lip and commented, "Look at the sky. How wide and blue it is."

At her silence he looked over and saw she was still peering out the car window. She was responding by looking? Or was she already aware the sky was blue, and it was obvious, so she felt no need to confirm his observation?

They drove the rest of the way in silence. He rode over the grid between the gateposts. The grid discouraged cattle from going over onto the roadway. And it eliminated the need to get out of the truck, open the gate, get back into the truck, drive through, then get out and *close* the damned gate before getting back inside the waiting truck.

Of course, driving in thataway on the grid, a man always has to peel off any woman who might be stuck to his chest. And she ought to be reasonably dressed.

There were cameras, which were triggered by any weight on the grid. A man, a horse, a beeve or a vehicle could trigger a picture. If anything went over the grid, it was filmed.

The film was evidence. The tape would show the truck, the driver and the license number. The cameras were cleverly hidden, but often stolen from their places. They were worth replacing even if it was a hell of a nuisance.

The cameras were for rustlers who could drive over the grid just like anybody else. And they could take out a cow or two and carry them off.

Austin looked over at his silent passenger as they exited the grid. He looked down her body. It was skinny. But there was potential. She was so nicely female. He lusted for her. He always had.

She'd gone away to college. He'd been twenty-four and thought he had plenty of time. Since she was then eighteen, if she wanted to be that educated, he could wait. Who could believe she'd be *married*—to another man—in just six months?

That was the first time.

Married and widowed three times, and she was now the age he had been when she'd left Fuquay to go to college! He'd thought she'd be safe there in Incarnate Word College. No men. The teachers were nuns. How did those three guys get to her so fast?

He'd find out.

Austin parked at his house, which he knew was now spotless. "Want to freshen up? Coffee?"

She didn't even look at him. She told him, "No, thank you. You can take me home."

Take her *home!* That jolted him. He looked at her and she was still looking out the window. Was she sick? "Don't you want to see the new baby calf that's just been born today?"

She turned big eyes to him and said, "Oh. Yes." And she looked out the windshield. "Where is it?"

"Down at the cattle barn. It isn't far."

"Okay."

They spent the entire rest of the morning at the barn. She smiled. She held a kitten on her lap. The barn dog loved Iris and quietly sat next to her, very alert and interested.

Since he had to do it in front of her, Austin was trying to think of a kind way to evict the dog and take its place. Austin knew he was too large to replace the kitten on her lap.

Austin asked one of the show-offy hands, "How'd you find the kitten?" Barn cats never allowed people to see their litters until the kittens could fend for themselves.

He heard another man tell Iris, "We heard them mewing. Their momma didn't come back. Something musta happened to her. *We—*" he moved his hand and changed his wording "—this one is the only…survivor."

The little ball of fur curled on Iris's lap and purred. The men exchanged glances. Any male allowed that close to her would purr.

And they looked at her. She'd been married three times. Their eyes narrowed and they watched her as they thought all sorts of things, but mostly how much money she'd have by then.

It took them a while, but they gradually realized that she was suffering. She was grieving. Then they looked at Austin. He was gentle to her. He wasn't just watching her, he was watching *over* her. She was his.

They frowned at Austin for being so obvious. He wanted that woman. That was what he was doing today. He was getting a toehold. He was watching over her and distracting her from those three dead husbands.

He was showing her a new calf, and a kitten was curled on her lap right where a man's hand wanted to be. Damn.

The momma cow was a milk cow and a pet anyway, so she didn't mind the audience. She licked her baby and it brawled and staggered and stumbled.

Iris smiled. She sat discreetly on the straw, out of the way, and held the purring kitten on her lap.

Her hands soothed and protected the kitten. It purred louder than any discreet cat would. Its purr rattled. It was safe there on her lap.

Austin watched his woman. When would she know that he was her next husband? How long would it be before he could put his face in her lap and purr?

The momma cow chewed on the fresh wheat grass they'd cut for her as a congratulations for having such a fine little bull calf. She watched as the new one staggered around quite well, and its bawl made a series of noises.

The spectators were all entertained...by Iris's reactions. She watched the calf. She occasionally petted the kitten. She offered no comment at all. She was simply there.

That was plenty for the men. More were there than were needed. It seemed to Austin that the barn was crammed with curious men.

Austin didn't object. It was a good time for them to view Iris and learn she belonged to their boss. To him. To Austin Farrell. She was his.

Of course, she had to learn that little fact herself. How was he to go about that?

Over on the back porch of the main house, the cook rattled the iron stick around the iron triangle to announce lunch.

Austin had expected the men to vanish. They al-

ways vanished to the house when the cook rattled
the iron triangle. However, while they were aware
of the sound, the men watched Iris to see what she
would do. If she stayed in the barn, some of the
men would skip lunch, Austin knew.

Austin went to her and held out his hand.
"That's the signal for lunch. Please sit with us."

As she started to decline, the men said things
like, "Yeah." "Stay." "The eats are good here."
"Try it," and "We don't mind."

She heard it all. She took Austin's proffered hand
and rose effortlessly. Even with the help to rise, she
appeared unknowing of the rest who were there.
She kept the kitten in her other hand. She curled it
against her skinny chest and smoothed its fur.

The men's faces were vulnerable.

The barn dog followed along as though he was
one of the group. Since he would make the house
dog get hostile, Austin told the barn dog to stay.

The dog obeyed. But the dog stood in the barn
door watching after those leaving as if he'd been
abandoned on a raft that was going farther out to
the sea.

Lunch was family style at the long plank table.
The cook watched the crowd come in and his squint
lines got pale when he realized a lady was going to
share their food.

That should have rattled the man, but he was a

cook. A real one. And without obvious panic, he made her plate dainty and attractive.

Some of the men mentioned they had their food slopped onto their plates. How come the lady got all that attention and they didn't?

While they ate, everybody competed for Iris's attention. They told stories. They ribbed one another and cleaned up jokes. The jokes weren't quite so funny that way, but they made her smile.

Her little smile was like winning a laurel.

Everybody there knew who Iris was and exactly what were her circumstances. Isolated people found out things and shared whatever they discovered. Gossip was paramount.

Lunch took a little longer than usual. Austin allowed it. Even the cook got a cup of coffee and sat down to listen. The story competition was a delight. Too bad somebody didn't tape it all. Some of the older hands told stories of long ago, which had been handed down the line. How accurate were they now? How much had they honed?

Austin was patient because Iris did listen. She moved her eyes to the one talking, and she listened. She never did laugh out loud, but here and there, she did smile at the stories they told.

It was like a gift, that smile. She was so fragile.

Austin knew that being here was good for Iris.

She needed to listen, not to respond. Right now, she could not. But she could hear. And she did.

He was especially pleased with his bunch. They were bent on distracting her. While calling attention to themselves, nobody mentioned loss or grief, but there was humor in everything if you just looked for it.

They told stories of hardship that were hilarious. They told about rescues that caused guffaws.

They didn't speak of love. Not at all. There were no quarrels mentioned. No deaths were allowed to be touched upon. She'd had enough of that for some time to come.

Austin wondered how they'd all known to censor their chatter and their jokes so well. He looked over his crew and knew yet again that they were superior men.

Well, for now, they were.

Actually, they were ornery, hardheaded, obstinate deadbeats. How could they be so moxie now with such a fragile flower?

How could they not?

With her carrying the purring kitten, whose head must be getting dizzy with its vibrating sounds, Austin finally took Iris home. She had given no indication of being ready to leave his place.

He'd wrestled with just keeping her there until

she said something about leaving. But how would her parents feel about him just...keeping their daughter?

Well, three *other* men had. She'd probably never even had a fling. They'd all just courted her and married her.

What about the second one? Had he just moved in on her? It hadn't been long after the first one was buried that she'd married the second.

It had been almost a year.

On the other side of his truck, with the cat on her lap in exhausted sleep, Iris sat as though she'd always sat there. She didn't talk to him at all.

He asked her, "Want to name the little bull calf?"

She looked over at Austin. "What would I name him?"

"Not Spots. That sounds too much like a dog."

She lifted her chin then lowered it to indicate she agreed.

Austin waited for her to say something. But she just sat there. So he asked, "What would be a good name for a grown bull?"

She silently considered. But she gave no names. She looked out the car window.

He said, "How about Bull's Eye?"

She slowly looked over to him. He saw the movement from the corner of his eye. When she was actually looking at him, he glanced over and smiled before he looked back at the road.

She said, "Okay."

Austin had been pushing for her to counter with another name. Now the new little calf would carry that name all the rest of his days. Bull's Eye. She'd never know how many jokes there'd be that Austin would have to listen to again and again. Endlessly. For the bull it wouldn't make no never mind, but for Austin... Good gravy!

Austin took Iris back to her mother and was pleasant and cordial to her hovering parents. Of course, he'd gotten there when it was almost suppertime and so he accepted the hospitable offer of something to wet his whistle. He sat and sipped his drink and visited so that no one could hustle him out of there.

Since he had settled in so well, there was nothing for the Smiths to do but suggest that he might stay for supper. It was so weak an offer that he should have declined, but he looked at his watch. He acted surprised as he saw the time it was, and he said, "Why...thank you. I will."

At the table were the middle daughters and the young son. And there was Iris who was silent. She moved the food on her plate and didn't join in on the conversations that eased around the table.

Her sister Emily was animated and flirty with Austin. She was twenty-two and worked at the telephone company office. Her animation was frowned on by her mother, but Emily ignored her mother's squinted eyes and chatted and laughed.

Sixteen-year-old Andy just ate. He was in that growing period in which he whipped down his food like a plague of locusts.

Jennifer and Frances were simply amused observers, and at times they shared hilarious glances.

Austin knew they were simply amused and not being nasty. Their daddy wasn't as certain. He eyed the two whose shared humor was especially sharp.

When dinner was over, they all cleared the table, and Austin did his share. But he didn't leave. He amused Jennifer and Frances so that their eyes sparkled.

The time went past and the parents exchanged glances. Austin gave no sign of leaving.

Edwina raised her eyebrows in question to her husband, but he shrugged.

However, at about nine-thirty, Austin did begin to leave. As he got up he said, "Well...." in prelude.

Iris, too, rose and said, "Good night." And she just left the room and went off up the stairs and was...gone.

So it was her family who saw Austin out to his truck.

Three

In the two days that followed, Austin paced and thought and groaned. He didn't for one minute think there was any way, at all, to get through the invisible, steel shield that surrounded Iris Smith Osburn Dallas Alden.

However, he felt the urgent need to see her. Why? Well, he…just…needed to see her. She was vulnerable. She'd already had three husbands. What if some other man got to her and convinced her to take *him!* Austin needed to be close to her so that she remembered him first.

But he seriously doubted that Iris thought anything at all about poor old Austin Farrell. She was oblivious of anyone. She was not in touch with the rest of the world. She endured the time that passed so slowly.

She was... Well, when Austin had escorted her to the play, she *had* watched, and she *had* absorbed it. Had she agreed with it? Now, that would be interesting.

Austin got his Stetson and went back to his pickup to go over to Iris's house to see her. Well, the house actually belonged to her parents and her siblings. How droll that he thought of it as being hers.

After he knocked once on the door, it was her mother who opened the door and smiled. She called to her daughter upstairs. Austin declined going into the living room and finding someplace to sit. He waited at the bottom of the stairs.

Mrs. Osburn Dallas Alden came down the stairs. She had on a different loose, long, carelessly wrinkled dress and her hair was not tidy. She had used no makeup at all. Even so, she was the woman he wanted to be with for the rest of his life.

Austin smiled.

Iris glanced at him in an uninterested manner. The time passed. She said nothing, so he didn't, either. They stood there. She finally asked, "What is it?"

"Come see the calf. He's steadier."

Without any response—at *all*—she walked on past him.

His mouth opened in shock because he thought she was snubbing him entirely. However, at the front door, she turned to it, reached over and opened it, went through the door and on outside toward his truck.

Recovering from his shock, and by striding with some push, Austin got to the truck before she did, and he opened the truck door for her. He stood there with the door opened for her and he watched her.

Again, Iris got into the vehicle without paying any attention to Austin.

He was transportation. That was obvious.

He went around the back of the pickup and got in on the driver's side. He glanced over at her as he put in the key, started the motor, and eased along, saying nothing. But using the car phone, he called her mother and told her where Iris was and where she wanted to go.

Her mother said, "Thank you" in a very tender, relieved manner.

Now…why did her family want her with him? Or were they just grateful that they'd know now where she was and with whom? He was the "whom." It was better to be with her, albeit silently, than to pace his empty house all by himself, just wondering where she was.

Iris said no word, at all, on the entire way to Austin's place.

When the two arrived there, at the barn, she was out of the pickup before he'd rightly stopped and gotten out to help her.

She just did everything on her own and without any courtesy to the male with her.

She was an independent cuss.

Austin hurried and followed Iris close enough so that he seemed to be with her. He hesitated when they got to the cow's slot in the barn. The momma cow had more room than any local human. She watched the calf and mooed if he was too curious. And her calf *was* steadier.

The new little creature was so curious. The three-day-old calf they'd named Bull's Eye still lost his footing a shade, but he could regain his equilibrium and was mostly frisky and alert and very nosy. He looked at *everything*. He smelled *everything,* and fortunately, no crawfish was around to snap a claw on his nose.

His big momma cow was tolerant and watchful. She mooed when the new calf was out of line. He stopped what he was doing wrong, but he did trip again when he thought he could fool his mother.

How typically male.

But he made even Iris laugh. He ate from Iris's hand. He nibbled the grain perfectly. His mother mooed softly once.

What had the cow said?

The calf stopped crowding Iris and looked at her curiously with jerking movements of its head. It was as if his mother had indicated that the cloth-covered creature was not one of them.

Iris laughed.

She *did!* It was she whom Austin watched. Not the calf. Calves were a dime a dozen. It was this woman who kept Austin's attention. He watched her, smiling, and a tear came from one of his eyes. She just might make it, after all.

Instantly, Austin tackled the problem of who all would eagerly help her to heal? Besides being a beautiful woman, it was the money she had from her dead husbands that lured the men. Men sought money, however it was found.

But Austin didn't need her money. He had his own. The problem was: How would Austin keep the eager mob of men away from her until she realized Austin Farrell was the one for her?

Then the little kitten wobbled out from under one side of the barn. It *came to Iris* and said, "Mew" in a very fragile manner.

Iris scooped it up and held it to her. She asked

Austin, "Has the momma cat fed him? He's hungry."

She'd spoken! She *had!*

Austin replied, "I'll look."

But he didn't find the momma cat. Knew she might never be found. And the new little kitten was hungry.

So they went to Austin's house and the kitten was given a dish of milk. Being as little as it was, it had trouble licking the milk as it was supposed to.

But Austin got an eyedropper—emergency feeder for hurt creatures—and it worked!

Iris asked another question, which startled Austin so much that he had to look at her to be sure it was *she* who had spoken. He then had to ask, "What did you say?"

Iris repeated, "Where is his mother?"

So they went out and searched the area for the momma cat. With the kitten starving, Austin had figured something had happened to the momma cat. The search was time taking, but it was a pleasure for him to be with Iris.

Then Iris spoke *again!* She said in regular conversation to him, "I'll take the kitten home with me and see to it being fed for you."

That whole, entire sentence!

He looked at Iris in astonishment, and nodded rather vapidly.

So *then* she asked, "Perhaps I should go on back now and begin to feed the kitten?"

Austin almost nodded, but he realized if she went home, then he would lose her attention. So he said, "I need to show you some things. I can carry the kitten while it eats. It'll be—"

But she said, "I'll take care of him. What did you want me to see?"

His mind went wild as he madly searched for a reply. He said, "Wellll…"

Iris asked, "Is it the flowers?" Fancy her asking *anything* right out loud thataway!

Austin looked at the tacky yard. The fields were perfect, but who had the time for the yard? The flower beds were overrun with weeds that hadn't been pulled—

Iris said, "I'll help."

That boggled him. He gasped. He didn't want this fragile woman to bend—

"I love flowers. Your mama did such a lovely job of them out here. You ought not let the weeds crowd them out, this way."

Austin looked at her blankly with no response at *all*. His mouth was open. She was actually talking to him! How'd that happen?

The kitten was out cold. It just went to sleep

lying on her hand. Iris slid the kitten into one of her skirt pockets, and she began to pull weeds.

So...Austin got a hat for Iris, and his mother's garden gloves. And he stopped Iris long enough to put them on. She smiled. She looked up at him and smiled *at* him!

He joined her in pulling weeds. He was astonished that he was doing it. But doing it *did* keep her there at his place.

Because she was so fragile and so careful, Austin was the one who pulled most of the weeds. He made her sit down and take the kitten out of her pocket for a while.

The kitten opened his eyes in a drunken manner of overeating, and he went back to sleep. Iris laughed at the sleepy kitten.

She pointed out the forgotten weeds, still there, that were so little they were just overlooked.

Austin was amused. She was picky. He watched her as she rested under his mother's big hat. And she held that damned sleeping kitten in her hands. She was so gentle that Austin was touched. She probably would take that kitten to bed with her. He sighed. Why not him?

She got Austin some water from the spigot in the yard and waited for him to come for it. "You need to sit down and rest a while."

She told him that. He laughed.

Iris watched him. "You need rest time, too. You've made me do it. I watched you. Your back is hurt. What did you do to it?"

He looked at her consideringly and told her, "We were pulling a tractor out of mud, and I pulled too hard."

"Dumb."

He grinned and nodded, fascinated that she could speak so easily now.

She told him, "Take care of it. Give it some time to recoup."

He slid his eyes over to her and asked, "Like now?"

She put the kitten back into the side pocket of her long, loose dress. She rose and said, "Show me where it hurts."

It was on the left back side above his waist.

She led him to the yard swing, which was six feet long. She had him lie down across the swing. His shoes were muddy so they were left hanging off the other end of the swing.

Then she pulled his shirt from his trousers and under the shirt was long johns.

He moved as he said, "I'll unbutton them."

But Iris said, "No need. I can rub your back with those on."

So Austin lay like a dog that had never been

petted and he didn't groan aloud in his pleasure. He only thanked God that he was front down.

After a time, she looked at him and exclaimed, "You're still awake!"

His eyes were bloodshot and he sweat. He just watched her.

She scolded him, "This is *supposed* to relax you so that you can sleep!"

He told her, "There are other…things…I want to do."

She misunderstood his careful speaking. She looked around at the tidied yard and told him, "You've done enough for today."

He smiled. His breathing was all wrong. He wondered if he'd be able to sit up on the swing with her still there. Or would he just gasp and shake his head and scare the liver out of her?

She'd had *three* husbands! She ought to understand men. Ahhh, but they'd been young and none had had her for long.

He asked her, "Do you know what you're doing to me?"

She smiled at him and said, "I'm very carefully loosening up these harmed muscles. You were very careless and foolish."

He wondered if any of her husbands had been careless or foolish around her. He wouldn't ask.

Then he thought how she'd changed in just that

day...finally. She now *talked* to him. Was it the cat? What had changed her? Was it working together like a...couple? Did she cotton to him? What woke her up?

But what if this was just something that was a similar happening with one of those three men whom she'd married?

He opened his bloodshot eyes and watched her earnestly rubbing down his back and side. The touch was won-der-ful. He worried that he was allowing her to work on him too hard. That she would tire and be bedridden for days.

He asked, "How did you learn to massage like that?"

She was silent for a long time.

Austin thought: My God, what have I raked up in her mind? And so silently suffered for her.

Iris said, "I was in the hospital for a while. They did this to my body." Then she asked, "Would you like your hands and feet worked on, too?"

He said, "Next time." He knew good and well he couldn't turn over, front side up. His sex was a very eager post.

She sat back and said, "Okay, you can sit up."

At least she didn't expect him to walk. He couldn't believe that she was chatting so easily. How could he continue the talking so that she would go on?

He turned wrong and put his legs out the back of the swing. She laughed! He folded his hands on the top of the swing back and put his chin on his stacked hands. He said, "What did I do to get in this trap?"

Again, she laughed.

He looked at her with his flushed face. He asked, "Are you through with me?"

"Your muscles are completely relaxed. You need such a rubdown each day for a while."

"I don't know of anyone else who does this. May I come over to you?"

"I'll drive over early each day until I can get you in shape."

She'd drive over? Then he asked in a suspicious way, "What time?"

"I suppose you will name the time?"

"Five a.m."

"*Five!*" She was appalled. "What are you having to do to get up at five?"

He sighed with tolerance. "I suppose I could come back to the house at seven."

"*Seven!*"

"That too late? Six?" He was still sitting backward on the swing with his elbows on the seat back. He turned his head to watch her, and he licked his lips.

She told him with a frown, "You shouldn't get up before seven."

He laughed.

"You get up *before* that...really?"

"There's a lot for a farmer to do."

She considered. She looked around. She said, "No wonder your mother did so much gardening. She was bored."

Austin was shocked out of his lust...just about. And he said, "Farming is a hard job, but time can be adjusted. Tell me what you like."

She looked around thoughtfully.

And he was again stunned that she was so alert. She could recover. He would have to fix whatever she wanted so that she could live there and feel normal. He would do that. Whatever it took, he would see to it that the living they did was *her* way.

Looking around, with the kitten in her hands again, she said, "You're a man."

He waited. She said nothing else. He told her in a husky voice, "I've noticed I'm a man, and you're a woman."

She looked at him and said nothing. Then she smiled just a very tiny bit. She said, "I'll take the kitten home with me until he's a little bigger. Then I'll give him back to you."

Austin said, "We'll see."

She gasped. "You don't want the kitten?"

"I want you." His mouth just said it.

Iris lifted her eyebrows and told him, "I don't hunt mice."

He replied softly, "Well, damn."

He was very aware that they were actually talking to each other. How astonishing it was. It rattled him a little, and he was aware that his breathing was too quick. He asked her, "What'll you fix me for lunch?"

She turned her head and looked at his house. She asked, "What do you have in there to eat? I didn't bring anything along."

Very carefully, he lifted his feet and turned, putting his feet down in front of the swing. He sought to breathe normally, and he slowly rose to his feet and put his hands into his pant pockets. He considered the sky and her and the house before he said, "Let's go see what's available...and you can call your mama and tell her you're going out for lunch."

"I'm not dressed to go out for lunch."

He corrected her. "Here. This is where you'll eat, and you look just right." Then he tilted his head and casually mentioned, "You can wash your hands."

She grinned. She *did!* She lifted the sleeping kitten and laughed softly.

That sound curled all his hair and stiffened his

appendages. He stood, turned his back and looked at the sky. He said, "You ruin a man."

She looked around and asked, "How's that?" She meant to inquire in what way.

Austin turned to her and said, "You're driving me crazy."

That startled her. "Why? In what way? What have I done?"

"I want you."

She looked at him soberly and considered.

He thought he'd spilled the beans and ruined *everything!*

She smiled just a tad and nodded as she said, "I could do that."

He shivered and gasped.

She looked around. She asked, "Is anyone in the house?"

"No."

She lifted her eyebrows. "Are you willing?"

My God! he thought. Willing? His breaths crowded on top of each other and he looked around carefully. Then he reached out his hand. He figured if she took it, she knew what she was doing.

She smiled and took his hand.

He was wobbled. All that while, and she'd been so zonked, and now she was not only *talking* to him but she was eager to love his body! Was it only…sex?

Well, if that was true, he wasn't going to deny his body this remarkable surcease. He might never have another chance. And he ought to know what those other three men had experienced.

He was jealous of them. Stupid. But it was true. He was hostile to them because they'd each... had...her. Now he would. And he'd *keep* her! He'd pay attention and he'd take care of her...and himself! He'd see to it that was so.

She looked at him and asked, "Do you lock your doors?"

"Yeah." He would. He'd lock her inside and not allow her out unless he was along. He looked at her. She'd get out a window and be gone.

He smiled slightly. "Love me."

"I'll share it with you. Have you done this before? As you know, I've had three husbands. They were all very kind and gentle. Are you?"

"I don't know."

She misunderstood. She said, "You've never— well, it's time for you. It's really very easy and very nice. I'll show you."

So *he* said, "Be gentle." He licked his lips and swallowed twice. His hands shook and his body was very tense.

She was startled. "You really *are* shaken. Would you like me to just kiss you now and approach this more slowly?"

He told her earnestly, "No. I'm ready for... whatever you plan to do to me."

"This is very kind of you. Being alone has been more than I can handle."

Seriously he said, "You want me?"

She laughed. "You seem perfect. Shall it be here in the unmowed grass, or would you prefer to go inside?"

"I need a shower."

Iris grinned and said, "I can take off your clothes and help there."

He watched her soberly, thinking of the times she must have done that to three other men. He was filled with bitter jealousy. He said, "So you've—" And his guardian angel stopped him cold.

"Yes." She teased him. "I'm...trained. I can do it all, and you can just lie there and endure." She laughed.

It was only then that he realized she was poking her head out of the enclosure she'd been stuck in with her grief. If he scolded her now, she'd go back into shock, and he'd *never* lure her out of it. Probably no other man would, either.

He said, "Do your damnedest!"

She grinned as she stood before him. Her eyes danced and her smile was a delight. She suggested, "Let's go over yonder under that tree. Then nobody can lean out of their gliders and yell at us."

He laughed, then hesitated. He asked, "When did that happen to you?"

She replied, "Never! But I did hear about it being done to others."

Very quickly, he distracted her as he said, "I'll cover you and hide you from any peeper."

She laughed as she looked around. Then she told him gently, "It's daytime."

"All normal people are working."

She grinned. "Only we're not working?"

"Are you gonna kiss me?"

She bit her lower lip to hide her widened grin. "I thought you'd do that first. Are you bashful?"

"Come against me." His breathing was very bullish.

She asked, "Do you have breathing problems?"

"Yeah...you!"

She was laughing when he pulled her against him and kissed her mouth so hungrily. He did a wonderful job of it. He just about wrecked her.

Lax in his arms, she asked, "How'd you...learn to do that...clear out here?"

His breathing harsh, he replied, "I've practiced."

Her eyes closed, she grinned, then she giggled and finally she just laughed out loud.

He could only think of how *different* she had become in that one short day. It was a miracle. Had she survived? Would she last until he'd tasted her?

Until he'd loved her? What if she turned and just walked on off? Did she want him as much as he wanted her?

He shivered as he thought of her seeking out another man. He'd see to it that she was surfeited, relaxed and depleted...by him.

Okay, he could do that.

He took her into his arms, and his mind noted how light she was. She needed meat on her bones. He lifted her and carried her over to the big old oak tree and there, in the shade, he put her feet on the ground. He said, "Just a minute."

She thought he'd run into the house and get a condom.

He undid his shoes and peeled off his socks, shirt and trousers and used them to make a bed for her on the ground. He pulled off the long johns and added them on top. She saw that he was fascinatingly naked.

She moved her head as her eyes looked at him and he was blushingly pleased and somewhat embarrassed. He *knew* he was well made. He told her, "It's only right that you discard *your* clothes if I have."

She did. She laughed and pulled off her long dress. She had nothing else on. He'd wondered. He was boggled and his breathing was strange. He couldn't draw in air or let it out. He was going to suffocate. But, by George, he was going to die happy.

He rolled on a condom, laid her down on the ground and slid over her. He said, "I don't want to hurt you. Put—"

But she was already doing that. Well, a woman with *three* husbands would have some— He gasped. His eyes slitted. He breathed through his mouth.

Her hands were on his hair and down his back, and she moaned softly and moved her body and about drove him right over the very edge of reality.

Four

Under the big tree in his yard, locked in Austin's arms and under him, Iris gasped and breathed. She said, "Hold still." She about moaned that.

He instantly looked around to be sure no one was approaching them—the two of them being in such a wondrous embrace. He tried to be still. He tried to control his breathing. He groaned and shivered, holding her under him and trying to ease his weight on top of her. He adjusted to allow her to breathe.

Iris did that. She breathed. She smiled. She put her hands in his hair. She said, "Let's—"

Austin went very still and shivered with his want.

He started to speak a couple of times and was not able, but he finally asked, "You okay?"

She curled her legs around him and made very wicked sounds with her smiling mouth. He saw that her eyes were closed. Who was she thinking about? Which husband? They were all dead.

Was she using him because of that? Was she pretending she was in one of *their* arms, under their bodies?

She said softly, "Austin..."

So she did know who was atop her and loving her. She did remember who *he* was. She moved under his excited body and rubbed her chest against him.

That did something strange to his ears, which perked and waggled. Never before then had his ears done any such thing! It boggled him a trifle. It would have been something astonishing but he was somewhat disoriented. He asked her again, "You okay?"

With her eyes closed and her body moving under his, she laughed so wickedly that he was somewhat shocked! He kissed her neck.

In a low voice she said, "Up here."

He slid his hot face up and kissed her mouth the way a man did. That was to reorient her.

She kissed him and his hair went straight out as if he'd put a finger in a live socket. Well, he'd done just about that, but not with his finger. He was...well...shocked!

Austin shivered.

With some startled compassion, Iris asked, "Are you cold?"

"I'm hotter than a two-dollar pistol."

She laughed. She thought he was hilarious at such a time!

He'd been serious. That was exactly how hot he was! A man seldom gets that involved with a woman's need. He wanted her to relish being with him. She was so nice in his roaming hands. He told her that.

Iris replied, "There's more to me than that. See?" She moved his hand on her. She made sounds and smiled, but her eyes were closed. Again she said, "*Ahhhh*, Austin. This is wonderful! I'd forgotten how nice a man could be to a woman."

Which man! He was riveted. He listened to her. Whose place had he taken? Which man's?

Slowly, together, their bodies climbed the magic spiral to eternity where they paused in extreme delight, then they spiraled down through amazement as they fell all the way back.

They landed there on his property, which slowly faded from being magic to being just a plain recently cleared yard.

Iris said, "Wow."

He was still stabling his equilibrium. Austin had never realized lovemaking could be so…potent. He'd been wobbled. Was it because she was so…skilled? Or was it because of the way he felt about her? How could he keep her to himself and not let any other man touch her?

Iris asked, "Was it good for you?"

"The best." Austin bit his lower lip. He could have just said, "Yeah," but he'd been honest. She *was* the best.

She was laughing. "So you think sex is a good adventure?"

"With you." Now why was he saying that to her? Austin hadn't planned it. His dumb mouth had a mind of its own.

Iris said, "You were wonderful."

Austin was stunned. Had the husbands been young, untrained and careful? Instead of jealousy, he felt sorry for them. To be so young and earnest at that age, and probably not know much. That would be tough.

Austin eased from Iris's succulent body and rolled over to lie flat, ruined maybe for the rest of time.

Iris curled up over him and put her hand along the side of his face. She asked, "Did I ruin you?"

"Just about." His eyes were closed.

She laughed softly.

Austin didn't open his eyes or turn to her, he just asked, "How many men have you ruined this-away?"

"You're my fourth."

That jolted him because she mentioned only her husbands—and him. His eyes opened and he looked at her quite seriously.

Iris was slowly rubbing her face on his shoulder. She shocked him. He was going to have to adjust to this and see it all as it was, which was probably just...fun...for her.

Austin's voice said, "I love you." Now that was interesting to hear himself saying such a thing. He *loved* her? Well, she'd allowed him the released relief of his sexual desire. His eyes squinted. She might well have to do it quite a few times until he could release her from his possession.

He asked her, "Do you feel as if I've possessed you?"

"It'll only last until you leave me."

She thought he was going to die? Well, he could understand. She'd had three husbands who'd done that. She probably thought all men did.

He told her sleepily, "I'll probably be around for a long old time."

And she said, "I hope so."

He asked her, "Just what do you have in mind?"

"I'd like you to take good care of yourself."

"Honey, I'm not only healthy, but I'm an iron man."

Iris replied in satisfaction, "Good."

"You...like...iron men?"

She shrugged her shoulders, which moved her skinny breasts, so Austin didn't at first assimilate what Iris said. She'd said, "I want you around."

He asked with some curiosity, "What caused you to warm up and talk today?"

"I think I'm coming out of it. And it was very nice to find you waiting. Have I misused you?"

As he lay on his back with his forearm over his eyes, he managed to say, "Not yet."

Iris laughed so softly and with such humor.

Austin lifted his arm and tilted the top of his head so that he could smile at her. He said, "You terrify me."

"Good." She put her hand on his face and rubbed it gently, then she used her fingers to comb back his hair.

He put his head back and allowed her the freedom of him.

Which she took.

He said, "Why, Iris, not that!" He gasped. "How intrusive!" And then, "I *am* shocked!"

She just laughed so softly and with such amusement. She said, "Brace yourself." And she slid up on him and put her little chest on his as she kissed his mouth. She did that carefully.

Austin put his hand on the back of her head and lengthened the kiss. His mouth was soft and his lips parted, teasing her sweet lips.

When he allowed her to lift her head, she exclaimed, "Who taught you to kiss like that?"

She'd never done it before?

He told her innocently, "I've had to defend my body and mouth from older, shocking women."

Iris gasped. "Wow. Show me what they did to you!"

"I wouldn't mind at all, but you don't have the...equipment...placed like mine."

"Oh."

"But...if you give me your hand," he said earnestly, "I'll show your hand what their hands did."

She felt shocked for him. He was breathing in what must have been panic.

She told him soberly, "You don't have to show me. But I'm so curious. Tell me what they did to you."

He was careful and very serious sounding. He said, "I'll just show your hand and you'll get the idea."

So he got to take her little hand and put it on him in startling ways.

Iris gasped, but she didn't jerk her hand away. She asked, "Did that hurt?"

He breathed. He moved her hand.

She was astounded. "They did *that*?"

Austin said, "Ummm."

Now...was that a reply, or was it...pleasure? Was he...intruding on her with moving her hand around on him thataway? It was marvelous!

Iris moved her head so that she looked at his face. He was somewhat pale. She asked, "Are you all right?"

Austin licked his lips.

She watched.

Austin opened one eye to see if she watched...then he closed it quickly.

Iris said, "I believe you're very sly."

"Yeah."

"How amazing. Do that last one again."

So Austin moved her hand as he wanted, but he pulled her body up and kissed her mouth in a squishy, naughty manner.

They did all sorts of things, and she was a very willing student.

The sun went down and the crickets woke up.

Iris gasped. She sat up and looked around. She said, "My mother will be so anxious about me."

"I called her and said I was taking you in to town

for supper." He'd made the call on one of his trips into the house.

"You wicked man! How could you do something so...sly!" But she ruined the entire scolding because she laughed.

"I suppose I'll have to fix you some peanut butter sandwiches? How hungry are you?"

Iris asked, "When did you decide I'd stay so long?"

Austin replied, "It was a hunch. You started talking. I wanted you here so that I could hear what you had to say."

She looked off and was serious. "I miss them."

"Yeah. But time has passed. They are gone. You have to let them go on off, and you have to look at me to replace their ghosts."

She was thoughtful and quiet. "I'll have to consider that. It wouldn't be too much for you to take me home now?"

"Aren't you hungry?"

"I suppose I'll come to that eventually. Do you want me to take the cat home?"

"It's so young that being with you for a while might keep it alive."

"I'll take care of him."

Austin raised up a tad and felt around on their clothing. "Is it around here?"

"Over there on my dress."

He looked at Iris. "I can't begin to tell you what it meant to me for you to be so kind today. Thank you."

"My pleasure."

"You aren't disposing me, are you?"

Iris laughed and shook her head. "I've never had such a time. You are a wonderful man and you're very good at making a woman feel special."

"I'm that different?"

She corrected him. "You're very skillful. I need another time with you to learn what lovemaking is about."

"Only another time?"

Iris looked at him and smiled. "We'll see."

He cautioned, "Don't discard me."

"I wonder if anyone else has the skill you do."

Austin was shocked. "You'd go around testing *other* men?"

"You forget that I've had three husbands. I am surprised you have more smoothness than they had. There wasn't anything wrong with what they did, it's just that you're more...clever."

He replied, "Yeah."

Iris continued easily, "I wonder if any other men have gone beyond—hush—you. If they have tricks that—be quiet—I might try."

Austin sat up in shock. He said, "Now just a minute here!"

So Iris asked kindly, "How many women have you had?"

He was belligerent. He spoke right off the cuff. He said, "That doesn't have anything to do with you. How old are you? And how many men have *you* had?"

Iris tilted her head and smiled just a tad as she asked, "How many women have *you* had? Tell me that and I'll share my own experiences."

Austin was appalled.

So she waited. And waited. Then she asked, "Are you still counting? That must be rather shocking, if there are that many."

He told her, "I don't understand you at all."

Iris wasn't boggled. She said, "Men very seldom understand women. The men I've known were innocent and considerate."

He was careful as he asked softly, "And I'm not either one?"

Iris smiled kindly. "You've already told me you're quite skilled."

"I did not!"

She explained easily, "It slipped."

"I would *never* have mentioned anything like that to you." Austin was very serious.

Iris responded, "You didn't intend to. It slipped. Don't worry. I'm not at all concerned. You haven't forgotten that I have had three husbands."

Then Iris smiled kindly, but she turned her head and looked beyond him. She was waiting for his protest. He was speechless. Sometimes men are that way. They get involved and never know when to stop and shut up.

Austin did stop. He watched the newly vocal woman and wondered just how those three husbands had handled such a clawed cat. Who would *ever* have believed that she was that knowledgeable?

It waggled a man.

He said, "I haven't had three wives. I've never had a wife. When I saw you, I thought you might take to me. You did, for a while. Now you're trying to pick a fight with me. Why?"

Iris was kind. "You misunderstand. There is no hostility in my being curious over who all you've…enjoyed. You've tasted me. I just wondered how I stand with your other women?"

Austin was positive. "None of them had three husbands."

"So…they didn't need the…experience…of being with you?"

He retorted, "They liked it."

She nodded. Then she got up and stretched, looking around. "It's late. I need to go home."

Austin told her, "I'll take you in the truck."

She discarded that. "No need. I can walk."

He told her, "It's late and the wolves are out."

"We have no wolves around here. Some dogs—"

"These wolves are men." Austin watched her as she tilted her head. He shook his slowly as he said, "I can't believe that you're talking...finally. I'm glad you're doing better."

Iris smiled at him. "Thank you for a very interesting afternoon."

He promised, "I can teach you anything you want to know...better."

"I believe it."

He quickly asked, "Now?"

But Iris shook her head. "No. The sun is going down, and I must go home. Thank you for this marvelous day. I can't tell you what it's like to feel alive again. Without you, it would never have happened."

He shook his head. "Yeah, it would've. You were just lost for a while."

Regarding him honestly, she told him, "You brought me back to reality."

Austin promised, "Reality isn't as nasty as you think. It's interesting."

"I didn't say it was nasty." Iris considered. "I began to share things with you. I am very grateful that you were kind enough to share this time with me. I must thank you seriously for that. I was zonked for a long while and couldn't make it back to reality. You did it for me."

Austin told her honestly, "I love you."

"No. You're just caught with the idea of solving a bad problem—me. You have solved me. Thank you."

He asked carefully, curious, "How are you... solved?"

She replied easily, "I can listen and talk and think. Before, I was lost in grief."

"Yeah." Austin did understand. "That's a good way of saying it. You were. But you've gone too far the other way. Now you're jumping at ideas that aren't true."

Iris laughed.

He found no humor in what he'd said. He watched her. "I just want you to know I'm glad you came out of it. That you can listen and talk. That you can understand what's around you. How soon do you want to go home, and are you prepared for your family to prod you?"

Iris considered. Then she told him, "I believe I'll wait until tomorrow."

"Tired?"

She smiled and nodded. "You're a fine man."

"I love you."

She shook her head. "I doubt that. I'm a different woman. I'll probably shock you."

Very seriously, he told her, "I can handle shock."

Iris tilted her head and inquired, "Would that 'shock' mean you jumped or that you shivered?"

"So you understand that you wreck me."

"Do I!" Iris exclaimed. "How nice of you to say that. I don't believe any of my husbands said I waggled them."

Austin informed her, "They were young and they were more than stunned. They couldn't believe that you belonged to them."

She laughed. She put her hand to her face and her eyes were slitted by her laughter.

He waited. Then he asked, "What makes you think they didn't gasp and shiver over you?"

Iris smiled a tad and inquired, "Do...*you*...gasp and shiver over me?"

"You saw me."

"I thought you were overheated from the hard work you did." She turned and put out a hand to indicate the yard. "You've done such a nice job of it."

Austin said honestly, "I wanted to do a job...on you."

"You did!" Iris exclaimed. She laughed. She blushed as she said, "It was so...nice!"

"Nice?" He was appalled.

"Well, what all can I say?"

"That you want more."

Her eyes just about closed as Iris smiled and said, "Later."

He gasped in shock without even knowing that he did it. He breathed through his mouth and swallowed noisily. He asked softly, "What are you doing to me?"

Iris was surprised. "I've not even touched you for you to complain about that now. I've left you alone!"

"Touch me."

She leaned over and put her hand on his cheek. "You were wonderful!"

Austin watched her with naked eyes. "You're saying past tense."

She grinned. "It was. How could I say, 'You are' since then?"

"I still have the same talent."

"You're a difficult man. There is no way that I can soften you. I've tried. You want different things than I do."

He asked, "What do you want that is different?"

Iris looked off into the night's beginning darkness. "I've been a zombie. How can I know what I want since I was just wakened...today."

"I woke you."

"And I thank you for that. I must go on home. My mother will fret."

But Austin was stern. He told her, "You're with me. She knows that."

"I need to go home."

"Stay with me."

She shook her head. "I need to go home." She rose and looked at the last of the sun's streak of light which gave her direction. She told Austin, "Thank you for bringing me back."

"I brought you *here!*"

"I have never realized in all this time what was going on and how I was. I need to go home and be with my family."

"I'll go with you."

Iris was practical. "I can do this by myself."

"You don't realize how long it's been that you've had no physical strain at all. You'd fold before you ever got home. How would they find you?"

She grinned. "I believe I'll ask if you will deliver me?"

"I'd be honored. I would have taken you home anyway. If I'd had to tackle you and drag you by your hair."

"Dragging me by my hair would have stimulated the whole, entire family to action."

"If you're hungry, you need to eat something now. I told your parents we were eating out."

Iris tilted her head. "Then I'd better have some peanut butter...now?"

"Come inside."

They quickly dressed, then Iris followed him into the house through the gathering darkness.

He turned on a light, and she realized how late it was. She said, "I'll take it along and eat it on the way."

So Austin made her a half sandwich because she'd declined a full one. But she did drink a whole glass of milk. The kitten was in her skirt pocket again and it meowed.

So Iris put the kitten on the table and fed it bits and pieces! It wasn't very old and such food was odd to it.

Austin watched. He wasn't chiding nor did he object to the kitten being on the table. Iris could do whatever she wanted. He just wanted her!

He said, "I could call your family and tell them the car's not working but you could stay with a cousin until morning."

Iris laughed. "My daddy would have a connip-tion."

In great surprise, Austin commented, "I've never seen one of those."

While she grinned at him, she said, "I believe I should be getting back home."

"You are so changed," he said. "What if you go out and beyond and I never can find you again?"

"I'm not leaving. I just need to go home. I need to be with my family."

Like any man, Austin's thinking was different. So he asked, "How about sharing with me."

"I have…this day."

"How do I rank?"

She considered. "Quite high. You are so kind." She smiled at him, watching him. She told him, "You're a wonderful lover."

"Could we do it again?"

She shook her head as she smiled. She said it again, "I need to go home."

"You've been living there all this time, and you haven't really seen your family?"

"No. I was locked in a phantom box and saw nothing."

"You saw the new calf in the barn."

"Yes." She smiled. "I remember that."

Austin went on stonily, "You sat and held the kitten."

"Yes."

Then his voice was gentle as he told her, "You need to stay here."

Iris shook her head, but she smiled kindly. "I need to go home."

"You've been with your family every day!"

"I was locked away within myself. Look at my wrists. I've lost weight. I wonder if they noticed that."

"We all did. Now that you're out of the withdrawal, let me be with you."

She laughed. "I'm already sore!"

"I *hurt* you?"

She shook her head. "You're wonderful. I loved being loved by you. We'll do it again, later, if you like."

"Yes."

She put her head back and laughed. "All men are willing."

But Austin countered, "Most are willing."

She shrugged but she said again, "I must go."

"I hate to have you leave me."

"Why? You're busy. You don't need me by your si—"

"Yes."

She laughed. "I want that in writing."

"I'll write you a letter."

"No." She shook her head as she laughed. "That's too obvious. You call me on the phone and whisper wicked things to me."

He became hostile. "*What* wicked things have guys said to you?"

"They were husbands."

His mouth went sour as he said, "I don't want to hear about it."

Iris chided, "I've already told you that you're more capable and clever than any of them. They were just not practiced."

Hastily, he responded, "I read books."

She laughed.

He was indignant. "Now why would you laugh at that?"

Yet again, she told him, "I have to go home. Either you are going to drive me over there, or I'll call Daddy to come pick me up. Hustle up and decide."

"I'll take you home."

She licked her lips as she tried to erase a grin. "How kind."

Slowly, he asked, "When will I get to see you again. *Everybody* will want to be with you and listen to you talk."

She moved her hands as if she discouraged mosquitoes. "No...no...no. My sisters will begin talking right off, just like that. I haven't listened to their problems or quarrels or any of the funny things. So they'll—"

Austin looked at the ceiling as he flapped his arms out and let them fall against his sides. "Everybody *else* will be talking *at* you. You'll go crazy.

Call me and I'll come get you and take you out onto the empty, silent land.''

Iris said softly, ''I've been there a long time. I want to hear again.''

He took her into his arms and held her silently.

Five

After a long moment, Austin told Iris, "I'm afraid I will lose you."

She turned and looked at him carefully. He was serious. She told him, "It was being with you that brought me out. I need to leave. My mother will be anxious. She has a marvelous imagination of disaster. I must go."

Iris turned toward the door and walked to it...as if to walk on home. He pulled the keys from his pocket and said, "I'll drive."

She turned back and grinned at him. "You thought I'd insist on driving now that I'm in touch?"

He sighed. "You've always been determined. I remember you at school taking control of kids and directing them."

"I did?"

Austin walked up to her and looked at her, reluctant to take her home, have her away from him.

Finally they went out to his car, and he reached her door first. How long would that last? He smiled a tad and knew he'd always be careful of her. She was so precious. She'd been so fragile. Now she was bursting from her prison and becoming herself again.

He opened the passenger's door, then got her safely locked in. He looked at her. Would he just naturally assume she would be by him without his having to direct her and follow her and see to it that she was where she was supposed to be—with him?

As he'd helped her into his car, he'd considered her. Women were so different. How come a man couldn't just say, "Okay," and that would be the end of the matter. After that, the woman would follow along if they moved. She'd do the chores and raise the kids.

Men had so many *other* things to get done.

Getting behind the wheel, he looked at the wakening woman who was so fragile. She was his. Did she understand that?

Austin drove her home in silence. He didn't know what on earth to say about the day. She'd come out of her cocoon...with *him*. *He'd* done that!

How?

He glanced over at her. She was sitting, holding that sleeping baby kitten in her hands. He looked at the cat and then at the road. If it hadn't been for Iris, that cat would be in some animal's belly and pleasantly deteriorating.

It seemed no time at all before they were at her house. Her mother and some of her sisters were immediately at the door...anxious.

Iris got out of the car and ran to them, laughing.

They were stunned. They thought she was crying! They stiffened and rushed to her and reached for her, while her mother called hoarsely for her husband, "Chas!"

Austin sighed and leaned his hands on the hood of the car. It was going to be a tough time as all the women jabbered and exclaimed and carried on...as they cried. He couldn't stand tears. He never knew what to do about tears. His own just leaked as they were now.

Chas came out, alert, and walked stiff-legged over to his wife who was in the mob of daughters. They were horrifically emotional! Chas looked at Austin who had his hands spread on the hood of his car and tears were running down *his* cheeks!

The car wasn't dented or wrecked on Chas's side that he could see. Everybody was on their feet. The women were all talking!

What the *hell* was happening?

Chas decided he needed a drink. Something to soothe him enough so that he could handle what all had happened. So, he went back inside the house and began to look for the Christmas bottle. Where had Edwina put it? Why did a man have to cope with women?

The others followed him into the house. He heard them. They were crying—or was it laughing? He needed the drink. He couldn't find the bottle so he drank a glass of water. It served as a pause.

Chas went back into the living room and watched the emotional chaos that ensued. He looked for Austin and located him, leaning in the doorway. He was solemn and he looked very tired. Austin was just watching Iris.

So Chas's eyes zeroed in on Iris with alarm. She was hurt? And his mouth opened slowly in relaxed astonishment. She was...*laughing!* She *talked!*

And his own eyes began to leak.

It was very late before the Smiths ever realized the night had passed into the beginnings of the next day. Austin Farrell was awake but sitting on the sofa. He'd yet to be trapped into saying even one word.

Iris was laughing. She smiled at the family. They could not get over the fact that she was alive and *with* them.

At sixteen, Andy was the youngest and only son. He was laughing with the humor he heard. He wasn't old enough to be bored as yet.

The sisters, Emily, Jennifer and Frances, were exuberant! They exclaimed over *finally* being able to connect with Iris. They hooted and hollered and laughed.

Their mother would say, "Not so loud." She'd say to Iris, "You need to rest. Don't overdo, Iris."

And the sisters protested, "Do you realize how *long* it's been since she *talked* to us? What if she doesn't have anything else to say tomorrow?"

Edwina asked the skinny, fragile Iris who appeared luminous, "Would you like to go to bed?"

And *she* asked, "With who all?"

That *shocked* Edwina into silence, but the sisters laughed and slapped their hands on their knees.

Iris then looked for Austin—and he was still there! She went over to him and asked, "Are you visiting or too tired to go home?"

He sleepily watched her before he told her softly, "I just wonder why you couldn't have stayed the way you were."

She laughed and shrugged her shoulders under that old long dress she wore.

So of course, her sisters all gathered around and insisted on knowing what was so funny?

Iris only laughed and never said a word, but Austin told the sisters, "You're too young. Hush up and go to bed."

One sassy sister asked, "Go to bed? With who all?"

Austin was shocked! He frowned at Iris and said, "You corrupting those sisters?"

She shrugged her shoulders in a fascinating way and said, "They were that way when I came back here. Who all's corrupted them?"

Three sisters pointed at the same time at Austin and said in unison, "He did!"

Austin was so shocked and *appalled* that his mouth fell open and he could not say one word.

The girls just laughed.

Chas came over and kindly told Austin, "Never you mind. Their mother has corrupted those females. A man never knows what women will say. It's a burden." He sighed with some drama. "I just hope I can get Andy to military school in time to save him."

None of the comments waggled Austin. He'd known the family just about all his life. It was Austin who'd figured Iris would get back from college in time to marry him. How could he have *ever* known that some yahoo in San Antone would lure his woman away from him?

Not only had one lured her, but so had *two* others! He looked at the woman and considered that he, too, had had her, that very day. She acted as if he'd been superior to those dead husbands. He found that instead of just being startled, he was a little cocky. Now that was true. He was.

How could he keep her from tasting any other man? He'd put a lock on her. She'd walk funny but she'd be pure.

Pure? After three husbands—*and* him?

Well, he'd make sure no other man could have Iris. Only he—Austin Farrell—would have the key to the lock. He'd make it a chastity belt like the ones the Crusaders gave their wives, taking the keys, then leaving England all those years ago.

The things a man has to cope with are all about women. Or untrustable other men. Nothing is easy.

It was almost dawn when Austin Farrell dragged himself away from the Smiths' to go to his own place to milk the cows.

Austin looked at the rising sun and wearily wondered if he would ever have Iris again. Would she be curious enough to come back? To allow him to make love to her again?

She had commented that he was more skilled than any of her husbands. Was that true? How could a man be...different? He worried about that.

He finally went to his bedroom to strip, and he thought to hell with all the rest of the farm, he'd milked the cows. It was the only thing that was desperately needed. The cows wouldn't need milking again until late that afternoon. He showered.

The reason he showered was because his bed was fresh. He couldn't lie down on it with sweat on him. And that woman had made him sweat.

But she'd bragged on him.

She had. Yes. She had!

His walk changed. He straightened his back. She'd bragged on his sexual ability! He smiled to himself and he slid into the bed, punched the sound tone on the phone and went into a heavy sleep.

At the Smith house, the females split and ran off to do various things they were compelled to mind. Some left the house entirely. Andy went to summer school.

Without any comment, Iris went up to her room, pulled off her dress and went to the shower.

It wasn't until she was clean and dried that she went back to bed, naked, and went to sleep. She had a slight smile on her face. The little kitten curled beside her on the bed.

* * *

When she wakened at noon, there was a note on the floor by her bed, put there by her mother. It said, "Well, hello! I heard you're back with us. May I come over about seven?" And it was signed: Bill.

Iris considered the note. Bill?

She stretched her body and was aware of being alive. How strange it was to be aware of life again.

The kitten was gone, but Iris had just about been pushed over to the edge of the bed. She smiled and got up. She went to shower again. She was *alive!* That was the miracle.

She hummed.

She put on a shirt and long pants, socks and sneakers. She went down the stairs to breakfast.

She found her mother in the kitchen.

Iris said to her mother, "Don't move. Have you slept?" She got the cereal and milk.

"This is a miracle."

Iris smiled. "It is for me."

Edwina said, "It is for us all."

Iris asked, "Why now? Why in this amazing time? I was ready to die and go find them."

Edwina understood that Iris spoke of her three young, dead husbands. She told her daughter, "You still must live. You must do something for others. You may marry yet again and have children."

Iris told her mother, "Your children are perfect." Her eyes twinkled.

How long had it been since Iris's eyes had twinkled? How long had it been since she had spoken so easily? What had happened that had changed her? Would they ever know?

Iris seemed so...normal...with her speech. Yet she was skin and bones. Would she be all right?

Her mother shivered. What if this rebirth ended and she was taken from them altogether?

Eating with relish, her eyes closing, her mouth tasting, her stomach delighting, Iris almost ruined her mother.

The problem for Edwina was that she saw reality...and she wanted to grab it and keep it! How could she? She would just have to...watch her precious daughter take this fling in her life. Would it last?

Ahhhh, that was the question. The heavy question that was unanswerable.

Their doctor hadn't even known why Iris had been in the lost zone. He'd had any number of doctors out to observe Iris.

Well, she was better now. Alert, interested, alive! For how long? Edwina wailed in her mind, *My God, my God, what is Iris to do? How is she to cope?*

And herself? The mother of this child? How was

she to ease whatever was coming to Iris? How was she to help her child?

Iris laughed and teased her siblings. She lifted the kitten and talked to it in a natural tone. Her brother Andy asked, "How come you can talk to that cat just like you used to talk to me?"

Iris shrugged and replied, "I must have been on hold. I never expected any tragedy to happen. It boggled me."

So Andy asked seriously, "How'd you get out of it?"

She considered how to reply. And she said gently, "I had lost three husbands. I couldn't handle that."

So Andy asked, "How'd you wake up?"

"I'm not sure." She went on: "It could have been the day. Or it might have been Austin. For me, it just happened."

"It sure took a long time. I didn't think you'd *ever* be yourself again."

Iris shrugged. "Oddly enough, it didn't bother me at all. I just...waited."

"So what do you think got to ya?"

Slowly, thinking, Iris considered. Then she said, "I don't know. It could have been the day, outside as we were. The kitten was there and needed me to help him. Perhaps it was being needed by something that reached into me.''

With his unreliable voice, which was oddly changing, Andy said, ''We needed you.''

Iris smiled and hugged him as she blinked back a big, emotional tear.

Andy sighed as if in release. ''I'm glad you came back.''

Iris considered those words. She hadn't been away...only gone? She smiled and said, ''Yes.''

Andy said, ''Wanna come watch us play ball? We're a mess.''

''Where will you be?''

Andy told her, ''Over at Charlie's house.''

''I'll come by if I can. I'm going to see if Mama needs anything from the store.''

Andy advised, ''My coach won't let us run around until we've practiced a while so he can know if we can or can't do anything. You ought to wait a while.''

''I have to see Austin. He was up all night long while the family listened to me talk. I had a lot stored up to say.'' She laughed.

''What all did you have stored up?''

''Nothing important. I don't remember anything I said, only that I was talking. I hadn't talked for—''

''A *long* time. We thought you'd quit!''

"Not yet."

Andy smiled. "Stick around. I'm gonna be the top ball carrier of the entire football team."

"Wow."

And that was what he really wanted to hear! He hadn't even known it. For his silent sister to be impressed was what he'd needed. He grinned. He laughed. He said, "You'll see." And he went out of the kitchen and down the steps, running.

Alone in the kitchen, Iris laughed softly, watching her brother run off to meet the others.

In the next room, her mother heard her daughter's soft laugh, and her own tears flowed. Just to hear *anything* from her eldest child was a miracle. How long would it last?

Having tidied the kitchen, Iris went out and took the car as if it was hers. It never occurred to her to ask permission. She went over to Austin's place and parked the car in the shade. Then she simply walked into Austin's house and called to him.

She heard him say, "Umph." So she went into his bedroom. She put her hands on her hips and asked, "What in the world are you doing still in bed?"

Austin sighed. He opened his eyes a slit and looked at her. He said, "Some dumb woman kept me at her house all of last night."

"It was I. However, I did not drag you there or keep you there. You were free to go anytime. I just came over to thank you for your patience in bringing me back to reality. Being alive is...remarkable!"

"Yeah." He settled down again, and closed his eyes.

She laughed. She did not demand that he open his eyes, but left the room.

He heard the door open, then close, followed by her light steps across his porch. He rose from the bed and wobbled a bit because he was still needing sleep. Then he heard her car start...and she left! She did!

That irritated the hell out of him! He stood there. She could have gotten into bed with him and helped him to go back to sleep. She just came in and thanked him for bringing her back to reality. He hadn't done any such thing. She'd done it all herself.

Austin went to the bathroom, filled a glass with water, and went back to bed. He couldn't figure her out. He turned over a couple of times and finally he slept.

Since Iris had had so few hours of sleep in the last two days, she went home and told her mother,

"I'm bushed. I've done too much running around. If it's okay, I'll just go back to bed and sleep."

Her mother gently nodded as she watched her fragile child.

Would she survive? Would she actually waken and be the same? Or would she give it all up and never rise from the bed?

Edwina didn't know who to turn to or what to do about this child. How could a mother cope? Edwina wanted to go into the closet, close the door and bawl.

Where was God? Why wasn't He comforting her? She needed support. She could not cope with all this odd change.

In the house, no one walked in shoes. Everyone was silent and careful as Iris slept. Iris was silent, too. She did not move. At various times, one of the sisters went into her room and listened and watched.

Iris breathed. It seemed shallow. Was it real? Did she actually inhale and exhale? Or was it just their hope?

Iris yawned and turned over.

That caused them all to leak tears and smile at each other. Iris was still alive.

Would she be able to get out of bed again? Or would she again be bed-bound? They would have to wait and see.

They had all spent so much time worrying about Iris that this new worry was merely a continuation.

They needed to wait and see.

Just before supper, Iris wakened, stretched and got out of bed! She did! She rose as if she'd done that every day! Her sisters crept silently into her room.

Iris smiled at them all and put on a dress that hung like a sack on her skinny body. She didn't appear to notice. She brushed her hair and twisted it interestingly, securing it with hairpins. She put on a light shade of lipstick.

Followed by her younger siblings, Iris went down the stairs and helped set the table. She gathered some flowers from the yard and made bouquets that didn't block anyone's view of the rest of the table.

It was no surprise that Austin came over just before they sat down to dinner. So another place was set so that he could sit next to Iris. They all accepted him.

Austin told the gathered Smiths about his lack of work that day because Iris had kept him up all night talking to him. He smiled at Iris. He put his hand on top of hers. "I'd forgotten she could talk."

Chas commented, "We'd all forgotten."

Iris tilted her head and smiled a tad as she said, "I'd just never had anything to communicate."

That made them all laugh. And they all talked at once.

After dinner, Austin and Iris went onto the screened porch and sat in easy chairs that were very comfortable.

Austin asked, "You okay?"

Iris grinned at him. "Do you recall my coming over and thanking you for the boost you gave me?"

"I thought it was sex!"

She blushed as she laughed. "Shhhh!" she scolded. Then she told him, "You were so kind to me. You took care of me and didn't demand anything in return. You just saw to it that I was happy. That momma cow and the baby were special."

"*You* are special." He watched her soberly.

Iris laughed gently as she said, "I love prejudice."

He told her, "After you finished high school and went to college, you were *supposed* to come back to me. How did you forget that?"

She was a tad huffy. "You never mentioned being interested in me."

"I was. I thought you certainly wanted to—"

"You were dating...what's her name. The

blonde at the eating place that burned out on the edge of town."

He supplied, "Milo's."

"That was it! It's been so long ago that I've forgotten her name."

He nodded and said, "So've I."

Iris straightened and said, "Hah! You went with other women."

So he said with equal irritation, "And you married *three* different men! As each one died of exhaustion from you, another was in line for the—"

"How dare you!"

He watched her for a minute. Then he said softly, "Were you...jealous? You sound so hostile." His voice softened. "All those—few women were just friends. They meant nothing to me. I waited for you to come home. And you did."

"There was no other place to go. I was like a wounded lioness. I needed a secret place."

He told her, "You didn't come to me."

Palms up, she said, "I didn't know you were still around."

He was shocked. He asked instantly, "Hadn't your parents told you I was here?"

She replied, "I didn't ask. I thought you were gone."

"I'm not married and I have no kids."

"I'm not married and neither do I have any children.'' Without even knowing it, she put her hands on her empty stomach.

Austin said, ''I love you, Iris.''

''Be patient.''

''Now what's that mean?''

''I need some time.''

So rather sassy and with a slight smile, Austin said, ''I'll take that under advisement.''

Iris said nothing at all. He watched her. Was she going back into the cocoon? He asked, ''You okay?''

''Tired.''

That one word scared the liver out of him. What did she mean? Was she going back into the darkness of oblivion? He took her hand and told her, ''I'm here.''

She leaned across the chair arm, put her head on his shoulder and was silent. That scared him spitless.

Why would she go silent again?

Six

Just about every day, Iris went over to see Austin. She greeted him with animation as he stared at her, still adjusting. She was alive? She wasn't just a mental wraith?

All Austin wanted to do was hold her on his lap. She was so delicate. He wanted to carry her on a cushion and save her. When he touched her, his muscles tightened so that he wouldn't do more than touch. He was terrified he'd hurt her.

It was she who took his hand and pulled him into the bedroom. It was she who lay on the bed and expected *him* to lie *on* top of her! He was just about petrified, and he almost didn't make love to her.

How could a man take a woman that fragile?

He loved her. It was the essence of her that caught him. She was so skinny that he was especially careful in touching her. His shoulders and knees and elbows held his weight when he was on top of her. He sweat.

She wrapped her skinny arms and legs around him and loved him. She laughed and kissed him. She hugged him and made savoring sounds.

Iris scared the liver out of Austin. He was afraid—every time—that she would die lying under him. And as accepting as he was, he wouldn't be able to manage to go with her.

No matter what all Austin would have done to go with her, he was too healthy and too solid. She would die, and he would have to live out the endless years until he could get to her again.

Austin looked at his fragile love and he groaned. She laughed at him. "Not again?"

He shook his head and held her so gently. He told her, "You're the reason my land is so tacky-looking. I spend all my time in here, pleasing you."

Iris was sassy. "Pleasing ... *me?* I was over here, so that I could drain you a little bit so that you'd walk better!"

He shook his head in denial but his eyes laughed. He was so careful of her. He held her gently and said, "I love you."

"It's about time you mentioned that. When are you going to give up being a bachelor and marry me?"

Austin raised himself on his elbows so that he could look soberly at her laughing face. He asked, "Are you serious?"

"How like a man to drag along, using a woman but not being at all committed!"

"I gave you a ring long ago when you were eighteen. You don't wear it."

She explained, "My finger shrunk. The ring is here, if you looked, at my throat."

He told her in a deadly way, "I don't want you grieving for other men while you're with me."

"Oh?" Iris asked as she lay under him. "Does that mean if I gasp, or cry, you'll think I'm thinking about someone else?"

"Yeah."

She moved restlessly. "Oh, for Pete's sake! You're jealous for no reason at all!"

Watching her face as he lay on top of her, his knees and elbows holding most of his weight, he told her, "You admitted your grief for them. In these last months, you ignored me and grieved for them."

Iris reached up and smoothed his hair. She told him, "You have no reason to be jealous."

He growled, "I am."

So she asked, "Then why are you lying on top of me and holding me captive?"

Austin gasped with some drama, "Is *that* how come men are on top?"

She retorted sassily, "No. They're on top because then they're in control."

He was astounded. He asked with great intentness, "Why, I thought a man always let the woman lie there and rest while he does all the work!"

As with all women who hear such male protest, she laughed.

With his greedy sex still embedded inside her— and finding that he always wanted to be a part of her—he asked her with softness and hesitation, "You like it?"

And she almost closed her eyes as she said, "Mmmmmmm," and smiled.

So he asked, "Why?"

She opened her eyes and looked up at him. Then she repeated, "Why?"

"Yeah. Women generally don't like a man fooling around with them like this."

She tilted her head so that she could explain herself, and he rested his chin by her ear. She told him, "All the chores at home are done. I've already seen the movie in town. During get-togethers, women say about the same things—every time—and they gossip quite foolishly about something they know nothing about. So I found a distracting, different kind of...entertainment?''

He laughed. And he pressed his sex more boldly into her. "Like that?"

She patted one skinny hand over her fake yawn and said, "I'll see."

He was so amused that he had to lie on top of her completely relaxed. As his laughter slowed, he said, "Ummmm."

She said, "Forget it."

"Now why would you be withdrawing?"

Iris explained, "I've been caught here for some time and I'm getting sore."

He moved his body carefully and rose on his elbows to look into her face. "I really thought you didn't mind. It's such a treasure for me to make love to you. I'm sorry that—"

"I like it."

"I thought you said—"

"No. I was teasing. I'd have complained and fought you if I didn't want to be under you this way. I would never have come to see you or to deliver anything here. I would have been more circumspect. But I think I love you."

He asked, "When did you find that out?"

"When we were together that first time. I've *never* had such sex. You're a master."

He gasped. He licked his lips. He stared. He was

wobbled. He said, "Somehow, I've never known about what other men could do."

She laughed.

Wanting more bragging of him from her, he said, "So. You think I'm pretty good?"

It was obvious to her that he needed to be admired. That he needed her to brag on him. How foolish he was. But then, she realized he had no yardstick for measure. She did. She had intimately known three other men. But how many women had *he* known? "How many women have you had?" she asked again.

"You."

"No other?"

Austin looked off to one side and finally said, "Not that I can remember."

She laughed.

He told her, "I like a woman who is free and laughs so easily."

"You don't remember having any other woman?"

On her, in her, propped on his elbows, his head lifted so that he could glance around and through the windows, Austin pushed up his lower lip. Then he said, "Not that I recall."

Iris laughed. Her eyes danced and sparkled.

He thought again how she'd had three husbands. From those marriages, she knew how different and special some men could be. *She* was the one who had known more than one man.

He felt that no woman needed to experience another man. Iris just needed to know him. Austin could handle that. He'd help her.

She said, "It's time for you to leave my body entirely."

"I'm the one who needs a nap. You exhaust me."

Iris smothered a laugh and licked her lips, but her eyes danced and her expression was naughty. She suggested, "You can release me and take a nap."

He retorted, "And you'd run away into the world and do what-all to who-all you came across?"

Iris promised, "Not…right away."

While his eyes laughed at her, he shifted his body a tad, put his hand to his chest and gasped quite dramatically.

She loved it.

He loved *her*.

She said, "Move. Get off. I need air."

"Picky, picky. Women are all strange."

So Iris asked, "How do you know such a wide range of women?"

He lifted his depleted body gently and then heaved off to one side. Then he reached out his big hand and rubbed her lower stomach while his other hand slid under her shoulder. He told her, "I'm not at all sure about women. They shock and baffle me. Hush! I believe there's a great man-drought? And, woman—now, don't you giggle over that. You asked what the reason was and I'm giving you my own opinion."

"Hah!"

Austin warned her, "If you sass me, I'll not control my hands, and you'll wiggle and squeal and carry on outrageously!"

Totally in control, she teased, "Yeah!"

He smiled wickedly.

She put up her hands and lifted one knee as she gasped. "No! No! Not that again!"

Amused, Austin said, "Some females just have to be shown how to behave. And I can see that— hush—*you* need some—be quiet—experience. Be still and I'll *try* to give you some direction!"

"Oh?" She was snippy and very amused. "Just what did you have in mind?" With a moan of pleasure she said, "I had no idea I wanted you again this soon!"

He cautioned, "Now just a min—"

Iris gasped and shivered and said, *"Now!"*

He said, "For crying out loud! What in the world is eating you?"

She said, "You!" And she leaned up and put her

arms around his head and nibbled very gently around his ear.

Austin told her, "Be careful. I only have two of those."

"Do you want me to wiggle out from under you and sit up?"

He said, "No."

"Then you'll have to be a gentleman and give me room. I'm becoming cramped under you. You're limiting my movements."

Alertly, Austin asked, "What did you have in mind?"

Quite easily, she mentioned, "Going home. It's getting late and—"

He said, "Hush your wicked mouth. I don't wanna hear about it."

"Surely, you don't want my daddy coming out looking for me?"

Austin said, "My name ain't Shirley."

So she told him, "'Surely' isn't a name. It is the beginning of a sentence implying that you aren't paying attention to conduct." She burst out laughing and continued with giggles and eyes that were filled with her humor.

"Why are you…laughing?"

And she replied in time, "I have no idea at all! I'm probably hungry and need to go home."

"I have food here."

Iris told him nicely, "I believe at home it's my turn to set the table."

"You could work on my table." He lifted carefully from her and fell onto the bed beside her, his hands still holding her where he wanted her...this time.

She smiled at him. She said, "I need to go home."

His eyes showed his regret that she would leave. Austin said, "I know. Kiss me once, so I can remember."

So she kissed him once...and he kissed her about five more times. She wiggled and laughed and protested...and he allowed Iris to get away.

She tidied herself, then kissed Austin goodbye and went home...leaving him there, watching after her. Insecure about her.

At home, her mother asked, "What on earth happened to your face?" She looked alarmed.

Iris felt her abraded face and said lightly, "Sunburn."

Edwina looked out at the overcast sky and considered. But she made no other comment.

It seemed that all the family was concentrated on what had happened to Iris's face. They didn't take to the—uh—sunburn tale at all. They knew the marks were from whiskers.

And Iris knew the family knew.

She liked the feel of Austin's whiskers on her neck. She liked it other places, too. Austin hadn't yet learned that. Or…he hadn't yet tried it with her.

Would he? She considered. He was really rather shy. Or would he wait until she mentioned him moving his face…on her? Time would tell.

Around the house, Iris did all the things she normally helped with, and she realized that her mother and her sisters were very careful of what all she did. They'd say, "Sit down and rest." They'd say, "No, you ought not do that." Then one of them would lift whatever it was.

Iris got to the point that she watched and listened and just went ahead and did whatever it was when no one else was around.

At night, she slept like a dead woman. She was exhausted and her body simply collapsed as she lay down on the bed. Every night, her body healed even more.

Iris wondered how Austin would treat a woman who was whole and okay. It would be interesting to witness that with her own body.

Yes.

It wasn't long before Austin mentioned, "I can't see your bones anymore."

That was an odd thing for a man to say to a

woman who was his lover. So she made him move off her, so that she could get up and go look in the mirror.

Austin turned over on the bed, put his arms under his head and watched Iris. He asked, "Where are you going?"

"You said my bones are gone."

"*Covered,*" he corrected.

Iris turned to look at him and lifted her chin as she mentioned, "My bones were under my skin. They were not so easily observed."

Austin was careful but honest. He said, "Uhhhhh. They were noticeable."

"I'll accept that." She turned back to the mirror. "I can't see my bones."

Watching her, Austin told her, "I don't believe anyone ever *saw* your bones, but you had gotten quite skinny. Come back to bed."

"I have to go home. They'll be concerned that I've gone off the road and hit a tree. They think I'm...fragile." Iris smiled.

Softly, he told her, "I hate it when you leave me all alone here...by myself."

"I'll be back." Then she brightened and suggested, "Or you could come to my house. My family would love seeing you."

"Can I go to bed there with you?"

Iris laughed and shook her head.

"Then I'll stay here."

She put on her clothes and tidied her hair. He watched and told her, "I'll be very lonely...here, all by myself."

She watched him watching her as she finished dressing. Iris told him, "I'll be back tomorrow to see the calf."

"And me."

"Oh, yes! I'd forgotten there would be someone here besides the c—"

But he'd levered himself up that quick and reached for her and dragged her right onto his body!

She said, laughing, "Help, help, help—"

That was when they heard the back door open and not close. Austin whispered, "Hush."

And he was so alert that she did exactly what he'd asked.

Austin whispered, "Go out that door and up to the attic. Be very quiet. Don't wear shoes."

Iris carried them. She was silent and vanished without a sound.

Austin slid out of the bed and made it appear as though he'd been sleeping alone. Then he pulled on trousers. Barefoot, he went to the closet and silently removed a very mean-looking gun.

Austin checked that it had bullets. Then he went down the stairs to the first floor to see what the sound was. He surprised the intruders in the kitchen looking for food. He asked, "What are you doing here?"

The two men looked up, surprised a tad.

But then a gun barrel was jammed into Austin's side in a very unkind way. And the gunman took Austin's weapon out of his hand.

Austin asked the gunholder, "You all just walk into a house just like that?"

One of the men smiled and said, "We're hungry and forgot our manners."

Another asked, "How come you're in the house, this time of day."

Austin replied, "I'm sick."

"Of working?" one of the men asked.

Austin said nothing more.

One of the men said, "We're starving."

With his eyes slightly squinched, Austin asked, "Somebody trailing you?"

"Naw. We thought on a day like this, it'd be silly to knock. You'd be out working."

Austin nodded. "There's always that chance."

"How come you're here?"

Austin replied easily, "How come you all came into my house without a hell-low?" That was two chosen words put together.

One intruder said, "We never figured a man would be indoors on a day like today."

Another man said softly, "I smell woman."

"My laundry lady was here."

"Where's she now? It's been a long, dry spell for us."

Austin corrected, "She *was* here." But the "long, dry spell" was a clue that the men had probably broken out of prison and were hunting not only for rifles and food, but women. *My God*, he said silently. *Help me keep them away from Iris.*

"Do you need food?" Austin asked.

One laughed. "So you're gonna help us?"

Austin replied, "I have food. I know what it means to be hungry." He went to the refrigerator's frozen top and pulled out steaks. He got sweet potatoes from a bin, and supplied other vegetables. He said, "Wash your hands."

They laughed. "Sounds like a woman."

Mildly, Austin mentioned, "Any man living alone knows to wash his hands." He asked no names. He simply wanted them out of there. So he helped.

Austin listened intently. Was Iris safely in the attic? Could she be still? One of the men apparently had scoped the house. He hadn't seen her? Austin prayed to God that she wasn't hanging out a dormer window and trying to attract attention...to save *him*.

Austin prepared a salad while the men sat, mostly

silent. Obviously, they'd had one hell of an escape. They were very tired.

To alert Iris that the intruders were still there, Austin continued to talk aloud. Surely she would know that the men would be able to sunder Austin. Surely she would be smart enough to be still. She was a woman whom these men would...use.

What if they decided to sleep there?

So Austin gave the men several ways to get out of the area. "Don't tell me which way you want to go, and that'll rattle the trailing men who will be after you. You ought to get out of here as soon as you can. You can tie me, and I probably won't be found until tomorrow about noon. Therefore, I need to eat and go to the john."

They listened to Austin. They smiled and said, "He's solid. He knows about people like us."

"Just stick to anyplace where the tracks are loose and there aren't many roads. Use a compass. They'll have a hell of a time finding you."

One of them said, "There's a little town near here—"

Austin nodded. "Be smart and avoid it."

So one of the brighter men asked logically, "How do you know all this?"

Austin replied, "I've had...visitors...before."

"Did any escape?"

Austin said, "You'd be surprised."

They laughed, then one man asked, "What is it that would surprise us?"

Austin looked at him clearly and replied, "How they got away."

So finally another man asked, "Any women? Around here?"

"Not here. I'm a single man. We don't have any women on the place because then the men would quarrel."

The men laughed and looked at each other. They asked, "Where do you keep the *lik-ker*." Not a question.

Austin replied, "I have very little—to use if a snake is nasty and bites somebody."

One asked, "How much is there in the bottle?"

Austin tilted his head and squinched his eyes a tad. "I'd say a wetting of booze for each mouth—excluding me."

They hooted over that. And they laughed at Austin for not getting drunk with them. He told them, in a kind and gentle way, "There isn't enough for you to get drunk, either, and you should be grateful. This way, you can go off in whatever direction you want, and you'll survive."

So one asked, "How do we leave you alive if we go on off by ourselves?"

Austin shrugged and gestured as he said, "You

tie me up, kill the phone and fix the car and truck so that I can't drive or call anyone.''

''I've heard that at the place.''

And the one saying it convinced Austin that they were, indeed, escapees from some prison. He didn't ask which one.

The meal was done, and the plates were put on the table. The men were hungry and ate voraciously. They were bent over their plates and didn't talk.

It was very strange, and Austin was tense, but he did eat.

In order to alert any of the ranch crew or Iris, Austin would say something every now and again, like ''May I pass the bread?'' or ''May I pass one of the bowls?'' or ''Do you have enough?''

But Austin was thinking: Was Iris all right? Where *was* she? Would she stay silent? Would she know how to hide?

God help them.

Seven

Austin's house was big. It was old and held treasures that were irreplaceable. The intruders didn't see those. They seemed to have no interest in anything but money, food—and women.

They believed there was no woman there, so clothing was their next concern. They were dirty and sweaty and needed a change. With proddings, they suggested that Austin lead the way upstairs.

In his mind, Austin pleaded with God. Where had Iris hidden?

On the way up the stairs to the second floor bedrooms, Austin prayed and bargained with God. He was sweating, but he kept calm. He figured he could get the advantage if the men didn't realize how tense he was.

One of them asked very quietly, "How come you waggle your hands thataway?"

In his mind, Austin was listing the lies he'd told them so that he would remember them. He easily replied, "I caught a calf yesterday, and my hands haven't recovered."

The intruders all laughed so easily. They had no clue—at all—that a young, vibrant woman was in the attic.

But Austin knew if they found Iris in the attic, they would be distracted entirely from leaving. All three? Maybe…just maybe two of them wouldn't. Well, maybe they would. Why had they been in prison? They were hardly pure if they had been there.

They'd kill him. And they might well kill her.

Before they did that— He shivered. He would protect Iris, no matter the cost.

Still heading to the second floor, sweating for the woman in the attic, it was very difficult for Austin to act normal. To lead the men. He talked to them all in a way that would clue Iris to what was happening. If she was listening at all, she would know.

He reached the top of the stairs and opened his

bedroom door. He said, "Here we are." His breathing was odd.

One asked, "You have trouble with stairs?"

Austin replied, "I hate stairs."

One of the men asked, "Why don't you find a room downstairs and sleep there nights? You got enough room."

Austin nodded. "I hadn't considered that."

Another of the men said snidely, "Mama must be in control?"

Austin spoke up immediately. "She rules." Actually, his mother couldn't have cared less.

However, the intruders took Austin seriously and they laughed.

Austin was silent.

With all the unkind laughter, Iris would know the intruders were still there. Austin bargained with God so that He would keep Iris safe. God gave no reply.

Austin opened his closet doors and said, "Take whatever" as he gestured to the clothing.

The men went berserk. They'd not had such a choice in all their lives, it seemed. And what they chose was interesting to Austin. However, as sly as Austin was, he'd been wrong when he'd assumed he would be able to leave. Under a continuous watch, he sat down and observed the men.

With all of them there, trying on clothes, they

didn't want the victim to slide away "somewheres else."

All Austin could think was—where was Iris? He did that with some odd care because he wanted her to remain hidden.

One of the men picked up Austin's golf clubs and looked at them. Austin said, "Be careful what you take. You're probably going to be stopped, and you won't want anything odd in the car."

Another man looked at Austin carefully. And he said to the others, "He's right. Listen to him."

Then the intruders got into one hell of a donnybrook over what they'd take along. They were red-faced and loud.

Austin listened with some interest because *somebody* might hear them and be curious. And amid such a vocal uproar, Iris might very well escape!

Or would she be so careful up in the attic that she'd remain still?

To hurry the intruders along, Austin asked, "Now where is one of you going to play golf? And how will you mention one golf bag with three of you there?"

"We'll split and take your truck, too."

Austin looked at his feet as he shook his head. He sat there and tilted his head as he said seriously, "Your aim is to escape. Don't do anything that will stir the interest of one of the TEXAS Rangers who'll probably stop you."

There was an odd silence.

Then one of the men said, "He's right. Let's be logical." That was the man who seemed smart enough to survive. How come he'd been in the clink? What had he done? Why would he risk being with such trash—just to be partially free for a short time?

Austin was silent. What had been needed from him had all been said. There was no reason to add to the comment of the escapee who'd backed him.

After the silence, there was grumbling. But the other men put back things that were too big to lug along. And the one who'd taken the golf clubs put them back. He grinned at Austin and said, "I'll come back for those. Leave them out so's I don't have to wreck the place in finding them."

Austin just watched the man. He didn't nod or smile or frown.

The crook thought Austin was scared.

However, Austin told them, "I'm not a cop. I want you out of here. I like the people on this place. Leave."

"Money. We need money for gas."

Austin considered. "I can get some together. The grocery batch. You can eat a couple of days on what I can give you in cash. A check would be suspicious. They'd tell you to come back in two days. By then, they'd have called the bank.''

That irritated the intruders.

Austin shrugged and calmly said, ''You should have warned me you were coming along so I'd have been prepared.''

While that comment irritated the liver out of two of the baddies, the other one laughed. That man should be given some sort of ease at the prison, Austin thought. He probably wasn't as bad as the other two.

The same man asked Austin, ''Why are you so helpful to us here?''

A good question.

Austin replied readily, ''I don't want my crew harmed at all.''

''You'd do all this for...somebody *else?*''

''They're good people.''

The man looked differently at Austin. The other two were all for slicing him up or battering him with rocks.

Austin was aware that his chances were not good.

Where was she? Where was Iris? He had no idea. His forehead was wet with sweat. So were the pits of his arms and around his waist. It wouldn't have been so bad if he knew Iris had made it out of the house.

Had he delayed the crooks enough? Had she had

the opportunity to leave when they were eating? When he took them up the stairs? How could he be sure she was actually gone? How could he look around for her?

All he could actually do was sweat. He was becoming very skilled in sweating. But his breathing wasn't all that good. Under his calm, he was jumpy. He needed to appear calm.

When he was set to knock out teeth and tie men up, how in hell could he be calm, though?

He worked at it. His mind sought things to say to them.

The one good man said, "You give us clothes and food. Why?"

"That way, I can get you out of here before the sheriff gets here and all hell breaks loose." He looked at the good man. "How did you get tied up with these heroes?"

The man smiled. "I got a woman who's itchy. She might become disinterested."

Austin said a soft, "Ahhhh."

"Yeah."

Very softly, Austin told him, "Break your leg and stay here until you can go back and finish your term."

"Don't tempt me."

Austin didn't move his lips as he said softly, "That is logic, not temptation."

The man smiled and replied, "Thank you." But he added, "It's all set up. If I don't go, they'll kill me...and probably you, too."

Finally, they were all dressed and ready to go. One of the intruders had filled his pockets with silver spoons, forks and knives.

Austin told the man seriously, "That's foolish. Who do you think will be misled by you having those? Look at the name on the utensils." It was Farrell.

"Well, hell."

The others became aware of the situation, and they verbally jumped on the stupid, collecting one.

One said, "Let him ride on the rear bumper."

"Good idea."

They were all so clean and dressed and free, that they were just a tad sassy, feeling as if it was all just about over and they really would be free!

Where was Iris?

Austin sat calmly in the chair where he was tied. The good man loosened the bindings so that Austin's blood could run okay. He said, "Somebody will come for you."

Austin almost smiled as he shook his head once. He did that to communicate to the man that he was foolish in leaving with the others.

One of the men slapped Austin's face quite hard.

Austin's nose and the inside of his cheek began to bleed. From the force of the blow, it was no surprise.

However, the good man was furious! He shouted, "Now what the *hell* did you do *that* for? He was tied. He wasn't trying anything!"

And the abuser asked, "Got a problem?"

The good man said, "You're a real bastard."

The abuser considered the comment and nodded as he said, "Yeah." He was clearly laying down a challenge.

Austin said softly to his protector, "Leave it."

While the protector didn't advance, the man stood his ground and watched the abuser.

The abuser felt that he'd won. He moved around as though he was above them all. He sought through Austin's things, making a mess of it all, but he found nothing else he wanted.

The men left. The good man looked around and said, "Somebody will come for you. I'm sorry."

Austin nodded once quite slowly. It was a twist to his gut that such a man was with the others who had no guidance, or suffered no pangs of remorse. Those others were not entirely human.

As soon as he heard the intruders drive off, Iris came into the room...silently. She smiled at him, then her face changed and she gasped. "They *hurt* you!"

He shook his head as he said, "It's okay."

Watching her intently, Austin breathed oddly. He hadn't known for sure that she was all right. He asked, "How in hell did you get down the stairs?"

She began to undo the ropes that held him captive. She tilted her head and said, "You were simply brilliant when you told me to get to the attic. You were so right! Thank you."

"How'd you get out? How'd you get down the stairs without anyone seeing or hearing you?"

Busy with the ropes that held him, Iris said, "I went out the attic window and down the roof right away. One of the hands made me wait on the roof under the tree limbs until the robbers accepted that no one else was around."

"Who else was around?"

She was still unwinding the mess of rope on him as she replied, "Everybody. They'd seen the rats arrive and they knew you were vulnerable. They wouldn't allow me to do *anything*. You'd have thought I was fragile."

Austin looked at her in shock. For crying out loud, she *was* fragile!

He unwound the rest of the rope and turned the chair toward her. He said earnestly, "Sit down."

Iris was startled, but she hurried. "I've left the engine of the car running so we can chase them! All of the ranch hands are eager. Here's a hankie for your face. Let's go." Then she stopped, turned back and looked at him. She asked, "Are you okay?"

He rose easily, casting the loose ropes aside, and he told her seriously, "You stay here."

She straightened and said, "Baloney. I go, too. I'll drive—you can shoot."

Austin squinched his eyes. He could tell that his men were her personal slaves. When he asked for help, they would tell him, "I'm busy. I'll get to that later."

They would be doing whatever it was that *she* wanted done.

Then he asked her, "How did you say you got out of the attic?"

Iris was startled by the question, so she said slowly, "I climbed out a window. I told you. We need to get going so that we can trail those men. Hurry up or our men will leave without us!"

And she walked right on out of the room and was...gone!

Austin ran. He caught up with her. He said, "Honey, st—"

And she said, "No. Be quiet. I'm sorry I loosened your ropes." Then she looked at him with eyes that actually held fire!

He was shocked! He gasped.

Again, Austin had to run in order to catch up with Iris.

Iris drove. The three ranch hands in back held onto whatever they could, and they looked cross-eyed and appalled by the manner in which she manipulated the automobile. She'd said she would, and she got to the action first.

The escapees' car had reached the highway to wind up in a traffic jam. Some of the cars had crashed together and were crippled.

If a person looked closely, he—or she—could see that the crippled cars were rusted where they had been crumpled.

That was odd.

An old man limped over to their idling vehicle, and they recognized him as the *grandfather* of the current sheriff.

He came to the driver's window and was delighted to see Iris. "How you doing, honey?"

But she just demanded, "Where is the car that just came from Austin's house?"

The old man grinned widely and said, "We directed them along the side of the road going north."

"North?" she exclaimed. "Why there's a stream under the road—ahhh. You trapped them."

"Yep."

Austin laughed. "They thought they had control."

"Yep."

And Iris laughed. So did the old man. The men in the back seat weren't amused.

Austin asked, "How many guys you got out here?"

"Well, you know how my grandson John is. He thinks it's only fair that anybody who wants to can come and join the party. John wants to go to Congress. He'll probably make it."

Austin said, "Yeah." Then he quickly added, "Can we take you somewhere?"

"Naw. I'm to watch from here. Thataway, the sheriff will think I'm safe." His old eyes twinkled.

Austin asked, "How can we get where they went?"

Leaning on the car's window frame, the grandfather said, "You can't. That's the reason I'm here. If all the rubberneckers got to go where what's happening, we'd have problems. You all can just go on back home."

Austin was earnest. "We want to help."

The old man smiled and said, "They get paid for what they do, and they know exactly how to do what-all. Now, I'm saving your necks. Hear the gunfire?"

They hadn't been listening, but once they were silent, they heard the shots far away. Their faces sobered and they asked, "Do they need us?"

"Naw. They've got it all figured out. Those bums won't last long before they give up."

Iris looked out at the sky and down at her fingernails before she mentioned, "I'm a little disappointed."

The old man laughed. "Lots are. I'm another disappointed one."

"You got to direct traffic. What if the crooks had decided to go the other way?"

"We have another crew yonder. So they could go either way."

Austin said, "I feel left out."

The old man smiled a tad and said, "Me, too."

So Austin and the others told the sheriff's grandfather to whistle if he needed them.

The old man nodded as he backed away from their car.

Those in the car asked, "We could help in moving the—uh—accumulation of old cars?"

The old man grinned. "No problem. Thanks anyway."

The carful turned around and went back down the lane and around through the trees to Austin's house. When they got to the house, they parked and sighed and slammed the car doors rather carelessly. Disillusioned, sapped from lack of adventure, they went into the house and halted, quite startled!

There on a comfortable chair holding a glass of

wine was one of the intruders. The man who'd been so different from the others. He smiled.

Austin asked in surprise, "They go off without you?"

Their guest replied easily and with a smile, "No. I saw what was obvious on the highway, and I didn't want to be one of those caught. So, as they drove along down the side of the highway, I suggested I'd just get out and leave them go on without me."

Austin asked, "What's your name?"

"Charles Bing."

Those in the room nodded soberly.

Charles went on easily, "I figured there would be some cops waiting on the car-blocked highway for us. So I got out. Neither man in the car was at all worried about me. They just let me go. That in itself was a relief. I walked over to a tree and watched them leave. Neither looked back."

He sipped the wine. "This is just delicious. We aren't given this at the prison."

With no hesitation, Austin asked The Question. "Why did you leave the prison with them?"

"I had a woman I worried about and wanted to see. It had been too long since I'd seen her or heard from her."

Austin nodded and said, "Ahhhh, I remember." Then he asked with curiosity, "Where is she?"

"I found out last night that she'd gone off with another man." He smiled wryly.

Austin considered the man and then said, "We'll contact your prison and tell them the other escapees dragged you along as a hostage."

Everyone laughed. But it wasn't humor—it was release! They figured out just exactly how Charles Bing would approach the prison personnel. And they waited until after supper when they told the sheriff that this poor, ragged, spent man had made his way back to their house. Yeah.

The cops came and got Charles. He was again in his very used prison clothes. As he left, they waved and told him to write them letters. He laughed.

The sheriff's granddaddy watched the wavers and he smiled slightly. He didn't say anything.

Austin was just glad that nothing had happened to Iris or his men...or himself. *Nothing*—and no one—would keep him from claiming Iris as his future wife.

Eight

Much later, Austin found the time to glance over at Iris. She laughed. She acted as if she was completely all right. And he wondered sadly if she really cared at all for him.

She had grieved so, for those three husbands, that she had gone into a decline and would have died. And here she was, smiling and laughing. Had she finally realized she was one in a busy world? Could she look around and see the sun and the moon and realize what a marvelous place this was?

If she could waken and see the world and him, could she love him? Or, not being able to die as she'd sought, was she just searching for a distraction?

Old fears surfaced. When she allowed him to make love with her, did she pretend he was one of the three?

He was a good man. His daddy had told him that. He was. And he'd waited *forever* for Iris to get to him. After three other men…could she love him?

When would she move in with him and call it home?

Austin looked closely at his woman. How much reality did she give to his being in love with her? Or was she simply using him?

How would he be able to keep her? What if she tired of him as she got stronger and wanted another man? My God! What would he do?

God was silent.

So Austin had to solve this problem all by himself?

Well, he'd go to her daddy and say, "She needs to get married, and I am willing."

That way, he wouldn't be on his knees, grasping her trouser legs, crying and begging.

Iris was a stubborn, irritating, wonderful woman. And she was curious.

How would he keep her curiosity and interest alive? He was an ordinary man.

She was his.

She probably didn't realize that and thought she was only using him. He was not stupid. He had her and he'd keep her, by George.

After a long time, Iris said, "I need to go on home so the family will know all the exciting gossip I've found here."

Austin sighed with a whole lot of endurance. "*Everybody* will hear or tell a part of the Invasion of the Escapees."

She smiled. "I need to get home so that I can tell the family the actual truth. Dragging the old cars onto the highway was brilliant."

"Yeah. Well, first I have to be sure to examine you and see that you're all right." She laughed, but she didn't move. He smiled kindly. "And I need to see the crew and be sure everyone is all right."

She replied, "I agree. So I'll just drive home. My car is just outside."

So he said, "May I escort you to your automobile?"

"I'd be honored."

As they walked to her car, he mentioned easily, "I'm glad you were here to rescue me."

She shook her head. "We were all around you. The only thing we couldn't do was use the phone in the barn or the garage. We had our cellular phones. We used those."

"That's logical."

She said, "Yep."

"Well, you all surely were alert and ready." He bowed. "I salute you."

"Without your having a cellular phone, that's how come the cops couldn't tell you what all to do and what all they were doing."

Austin said thoughtfully, "If they would have called on the phone, it was one of the intruders who would've answered the phone."

She explained: "Under those…conditions, the cops would have said a tornado was on the way and to take shelter!"

He was indignant. "I'd have been in a shelter with those bastards?"

She shrugged. "They'd have tried to run away, but the cops would have tagged them."

Austin nodded. "If the escapees hadn't left in one of my cars, the cops would have come in as line stringers or checked cattle brandings or something like that."

She asked in surprise, "How many times have you had intruders?"

"Only a couple of times that I recall. I've been tied up and left, but it's never been for long."

"Good gravy!"

He told her, "You all were brilliant. You stayed and called the cops—and *you* were foolishly around directing the others." Then he told her kindly, "I could have handled it alone. The only problem was keeping you safe…and away from their greedy hands.''

She looked at him with endurance and scoffed, ''I'm only attractive to you.''

He watched her. He said softly, ''You foolish, foolish woman.''

That stiffened her. ''How can you call me foolish?''

''You believe that you're only attractive to me. Don't you see the other men who look at you with wiped-out faces as if they'd never seen anything like you before?''

She told him, ''They're shocked I'm so skinny.''

He shook his head. ''No, honey, you're magic.''

She laughed and thought he was hilarious. Very charming. That was probably because she allowed him her body.

He was silent as he watched her.

She reached up and kissed his mouth. She was going to leave. It was a goodbye.

He accepted that. But he didn't take her against him. He knew the crew watched. They didn't need to know how much he cared for her. What he needed to do was to get the work done, and the men gone, so that he could have her alone.

With him.

Being a lover was a real problem. A man never

had the time or the eagerness to do all the other chores. Not that *she* was a chore! How had he ever found her?

"How'd I find you?" he asked aloud.

She smiled and replied, "I'll see you when everything cools...including you."

He put his lower lip under his teeth to prevent a smile and that way he thought he looked pensive.

She sighed. Then she turned and walked over to her own car.

He followed. "You haven't kissed me goodbye."

"I've kissed you much too much with all the crew peeking out from behind finger-curled shades." She didn't even stop and face him. She just muttered all that.

He was indignant. "That's not true!"

Reaching her car door, she opened it as she looked at him with a forbearing that was shocking.

He straightened and said seriously, "If I annoy you—" Then he realized what he was saying, so he finished differently, "I beg your pardon."

She laughed as she got into her car, closed the door and pushed down the door lock. She put in the key and started the car.

He approached the car, leaned over and moved his mouth as if he was saying something.

She saw that in the sideview mirror. She looked

up at him and her eyes danced with humor. She just drove away, turning at the side of the barn.

He stood and watched after her, putting his hands into his pockets.

Why would she leave without finding out whether or not she could get across the highway and go on into town? Women were, at best, very difficult.

He went and called the highway patrol and inquired about the highway. They said with patience, "It's okay. Slower, but all right."

He said, "Thank you."

"Sure."

And Austin hung up the phone. So she'd get home all right. He needed to marry Iris to get a better grip on her conduct.

On the highway, with all the doors locked and the windows up, Iris drove carefully as directed by the crew that was removing the dead cars they'd put into place.

Iris began to understand what all the cops had gone through to help Austin. She wondered if he realized just how intense and careful all those people had been in saving Austin's neck? She was grateful. She shivered as she realized all that had been done to save him. And she also realized how

calm he'd been and how carefully he had seen to it
that *she* was all right.

Austin would be that way with children. He
would work himself to a nub, to see to it that anyone needing him would be all right.

Iris would marry him. Yeah. She really would.
A fourth try. What would her three dead husbands
think? Austin would take some hard training, but
she thought she was capable in managing that.

Back home, Austin was considering how he
could train Iris so that she would be easier to control. He was exhausted in trying to help her out and
see to it that she was safe.

Iris was a hell of a problem. Were all women
that way? He tried to think over all the women he'd
had to tackle—well, not actually, but those with
whom he'd had to cope. It had started when he was
about twelve, and it was mostly his mother.

His dad had apparently given up on his wife. He
never did anything about her! He just allowed her
to figure it all out and do whatever she wanted.

That was when Austin started to help with his
mother. His dad and mom said he intruded. Inter-
fered. He figured they were both difficult and
strange…and his dad was not paying attention.

His mother was just lucky she'd had a son like
him who'd watch things and help out and direct.

Suddenly, Austin remembered hearing his two parents sniggle and giggle late at night in their bedroom down the hall! Hmmmm.

It was taking him a long old time to understand that *nobody* needed any guidance from him. How odd for him to realize that.

So he wasn't the King of the Road? He wasn't the one in charge? Now that was droll. How had they all endured him? Why hadn't one of them mentioned to him to back off and leave them alone?

So he called his mother and said, "This is your son, Austin. I've changed. I'm allowing people to do as they choose. I beg your pardon."

Then, typically giving her no chance to reply, he hung up the phone and felt...adult. So *this* was what an adult felt? That he was in control, not of other people, but of himself?

So he called Iris, but she wasn't home yet.

He would call her again, later. Perhaps they would discuss what all she had in mind to do. She would be free.

Where the *hell* was she and why?

Women weren't made to monitor themselves. They needed a man to control them and to direct them. He thought again that his father was too lenient with his mother.

Austin was somewhat startled to find himself

thinking along another line. He needed to be calm. He carefully dialed Iris's number.

She didn't answer her phone. Where was she? She'd had time to get home by then. She'd said she was driving home.

Well, maybe she'd stopped at a grocery store. God only knew what a woman would do all by herself.

And the niggle came as he recalled that she'd locked her car door. She'd done that to keep him away from her. She was going to leave. She thought she could decide what she wanted to do.

Women were thataway. A man was calm and considerate, but he did control.

Where the hell *was* she?

He dialed again. There was no answer. She'd been in a wreck? She was a good driver. One of her husbands had taught her to drive. It was her first husband. Damn.

Austin had some issue with becoming her fourth husband: that he was rather late getting to her. He thought of all the ways those husbands had influenced her. He would have a hell of a time trying to control her.

Just today, she'd locked the car door so that he couldn't open it and get her out. She'd wanted to go home. And she'd done that.

Who was in control here?

He was.

Well, at least he was trying.

He called her again. No answer.

That about blew off the top of Austin's head. He looked at the phone, which was useless. And he hung it up.

So Austin went outside and walked with the dog—actually, the dog came alongside and walked with him. Everything was calm—except Austin. The sky was beautiful. It had been a long old day.

He straightened and thought of what a strange day it had been. He wondered how Charles Bing was doing at prison. He wondered if Charles was calm and easy.

Of course, *he* wasn't—not Austin Farrell. He'd discovered that women were harder to control than he'd figured.

So he remembered back to the women he'd courted. He'd been careful and kind, but they had left him. He'd never realized exactly why. He only knew they left and he didn't grieve too much over them.

He realized that none of the breakups he'd had with women had been his doing. It had been the women who'd decided to leave him. He was too dominating.

That was such a shock to him. He only felt male and in control. Iris had been so fragile that he had been very careful of her. Any woman who'd lost three husbands could well be very cautious about marrying another man.

Was she careful of him? Or was she abandoning men because she'd found them frail?

Frail! She was skin and bones. But she loved being loved.

Had she exhausted and worn out the three? Is that what really happened to them? It was a remarkable way to go, but maybe she was different now. She'd made love with him, and it had been normal. Maybe she was more careful now that she was older?

Her first husband had died in a war abroad. Her second had died of some plague abroad, and the third had been killed by a loose bull. She hadn't been the killer of any of them.

So Iris was innocent. She was fragile. Her body was hungry for Austin, now. Had she been that way with the husbands? It didn't matter. He loved her. He wanted her with him. It wasn't just sex.

He needed to be careful of her. Again, he recalled that she'd locked her car door and insisted on going home.

Was she withdrawing from him? Had she only pretended that she liked making love with him?

Austin was a walker, fortunately. He looked at

all the stables and barns, the corrals and pastures. He watched the sky darken with the night.

He was restless.

He went back into the empty house and listened to the silence. He was alone. He turned on the TV and listened to the news.

He called Iris and she answered the phone! He asked, "You okay?"

"What a traffic jam! *Everybody* wanted to honk their horns and get out of their cars. All because of the pileup to stop the inmates from getting away."

"They didn't?"

"Of course not."

"Are you okay?"

"I'm furious and irritated and everybody here at home is treating me as if I am fragile."

In a low voice, he said seriously, "You are."

"Fragile?"

"Perfect."

"My family is spoiling me rotten. I'll get used to it and expect you to act the same way."

"Okay."

"Hah! I'll get that on tape and rub your nose in it."

"Come to my house. It's—"

"I wouldn't go out on that highway again for *anything!* Take a cold bath."

And he heard her hang up!

Well, he'd give her this time to herself now. Because before long, he'd make sure he never let her go.

Nine

So Iris Smith Osburn Dallas Alden, who was twenty-four years old, had given Austin succinct directions. Austin Farrell was to take a cold shower and go to bed. That was logical.

Being male, he then looked at the western area where the cowardly sun had fled to hide. He was left there after such a day? Alone? No one was around to hold his hand and comfort him.

That was one problem—of many—that a man had to accept. Women thought men were able to cope with whatever happened. The man had serious trouble if he gasped in shock or cried over some tragedy. It was the stiff upper lip thing.

Well, if Austin felt vulnerable, why did he assume that a woman needed a man to protect her?

He'd seen men mistreat women who protested and fought. He'd intervened. Several different times the woman then fought Austin off her man! And it had been she who had protected the bastard who'd been mistreating her!

People were strange.

One of the dogs sat close to Austin. The dog wasn't smiling or panting. It sat with a closed mouth and just looked around.

Austin decided to share some knowledge with the dog whose name was Yip. He told Yip, "All females should be kept in places like the old harems. Isolated from other males. Not allowed to go anywhere alone." He shifted and looked at the rising moon pensively.

There was a howl off some distance.

Austin asked Yip, "That a male looking for a female?"

The dog smiled before he went off at a gallop. Ears up. Gone.

Austin muttered, "That's undoubtedly a male gathering." He nodded to himself, for no one else was anywhere around.

Austin sighed heavily and walked slowly back to the house. There on the porch swing was...a woman. It was Iris.

He did not gasp or move in elaborate shock. He walked slowly toward the swing, with his head down. He was being the soul of a discarded man. With his hands in his pants pockets, he sighed forlornly.

She giggled.

He whipped his head up as if in shock! His hands came out of his pockets and he crouched dramatically, as if he was about to be attacked! He looked over at the giggling woman and gasped! Then he slowly straightened as she smothered her laughter. He asked, "Is that you?"

And she replied, "Who're you looking for to turn up?"

So he said, "Well, thank God you aren't—" Then his voice changed into stilted courtesy. "Well, hello—uh—Iris...isn't it?"

She loved it. He'd really expected her to be indignant and hostile. But she softly laughed in amusement.

He went over to her slowly, his hands back in his pants pockets. And the damned dog came back. The dog was instantly alert and he growled at the female intruder.

Iris thought that was hilarious, too, and she just laughed. She expected Austin to soothe the dog.

He told the dog, "Stay." So Austin hadn't told the dog to calm down and go away. He had it sit and watch her. If she moved, the dog would counter her and keep her where she was.

Knowing dogs, Iris sighed with tolerance and said, "Okay, call him off."

Indignant, Austin inquired, "In the dark, how do I know who you are and why you're here? Explain yourself, woman."

"If you weren't so dramatic, I'd probably go on home again. The highways are clear now."

"So you came back to check them out?"

"No. I came back to you."

"For what?"

On the swing, she shrugged her shoulders in a way that was eye-appealing. She said, "I found that I wanted to be with you."

"Why?"

That was an interesting question. She was hesitant to reply. But she finally smiled at him and repeated, "I wanted to be with you."

Again, he asked, "Why?"

So Iris said, "I've looked around for about twenty years now and I've found—"

Austin interrupted. "Since you were four? You've been looking for a man since you were *four*?"

She sighed in rather elaborate forbearance. "You're interrupting."

"Oh, sorry. What were you saying?"

"Uhhhh. How far had I gotten?"

Austin exclaimed, "You'd been 'looking around for twenty—'"

"Yes—years." She lifted a staying hand and told him, "And you're all I've been able to find around these here parts." Her big, sad eyes looked off into the night as she sighed.

He was indignant. She was complaining? She'd had three husbands! Was her body greedy? Yeah. She was after another man—him.

He faced reality and understood that he would have to take care of her. He'd just have to cope.

Austin sighed rather dramatically, jammed his hands deeper into his trouser pockets and was stern with his eager body, which was willing. Ready. Anxious. Ah, hell. She had him in the palm of her hand.

He went over and put his hands under her armpits and lifted her skinny body right up and along his. She was so light, he could do anything with her very easily. He growled at her, "Don't gain any more weight."

Iris laughed softly and asked, "I'm getting too heavy for you, darling?"

"Be quiet."

"Uhhhh…"

"Hush."

"Yes, sir."

Austin growled, "That's better." So he kissed her mouth in a very, very subtle, maddening way. He was gentle and serious. He prolonged the kiss.

She wobbled.

He grinned inside with his face still serious. He knew how to wobble women. He was in control.

Iris put her hands on either side of his head and she held his head where she wanted it. Then she kissed him, and his mind blew.

Just like that!

When Iris finally released Austin's mouth from a kiss that shivered his insides, she just ignored the fact that her fragile body was leaning against his chest and stomach. She managed to tilt her head back and with some effort she lifted her eyelids.

His eyes were on hers and Austin was in shock! She'd lured him, but she'd never before done *that* to him! He was wobbled.

He stood there holding Iris gently so that she wouldn't slide right on down him and become a puddle on the ground. That was just not grown male conduct. And he was astonished that his body could function automatically.

Austin said, "Let's go inside."

How automatic and how male.

Slowly Iris found that she could move her head. She said, "Okay." Then she wondered what she'd agreed to? She considered and couldn't figure it out so she shrugged.

In the lengthening silence, Iris finally decided she'd find out one way or the other. She just couldn't drive home—not right away. Right then, she wasn't sure exactly how to steer the car.

She was tugged toward the door, and as stunned as she was, she allowed Austin to take her into his lair. She was already familiar with it. She smiled.

Inside, he took her up the stairs to his room. How simple. He opened the door and saw to it that she managed to walk across the threshold and into the room.

Unbuttoning his shirt, Austin went over to the bed and lifted back the covers. He smiled at her.

She allowed that. She pretended that she couldn't reach the hooks that held her gown. She struggled.

Taking off his shirt, he said, "Let me."

It was interesting to notice how he neglected to get out of his clothes as he monitored how she got out of hers. He reminded her, "You've done that before."

She laughed.

"Who all's watched you undress?"

She looked at him with lowered eyelids. She said softly, "You."

"Who else?"

She replied with raised eyebrows. "My overnight girlfriends?"

"No...men?"

"My husbands."

That was obvious so he went on. "Who else?"

"We're still only saying men?"

"Yeah."

She considered. "Not even the doctor watches that."

"That proves he's smart."

"I believe he's just terribly busy."

Austin laughed softly, his eyes brimming with delight as he watched her. He asked, "Are you going to finish getting rid of the stuff on you now?"

"I suppose. I'd hate for this gown to get crumpled."

"Yeah." He grinned, and his eyes were so hot it was amazing they didn't start a fire in his eyelashes then eyebrows and finally his hair!

So she took the gown all the way off.

She wore nothing under it.

That wobbled him considerably.

Why would he be surprised? She'd been thataway the first time they'd made love.

She hadn't removed her shoes. So she again stood there with her gown held in front, almost covering her, but still wearing the high heels.

He said, "I'll hang that gown on a hanger for you."

She replied, "How kind."

This was the woman who had just about abandoned him not very long ago on that very night.

He silently chortled. That wasn't easy, doing it silently.

He hung up her gown, but it had taken a while for his head to turn to help his hand find the hanger in the closet. He couldn't take his eyes off her. It was a nuisance to move his eyes and find a hanger.

How many times, by that night, had the two of them made love? Enough times that he ought not be *that* boggled. He knew women. *She* didn't realize how many women he'd known. But at his age, she ought not consider him a neophyte.

Finally he got the dress hung up in his closet, and he was already almost instantly naked. He said to her yet again, "Don't believe it's the size it is?"

"I *do* wonder."

Austin said carefully, "You already know you can handle it."

She watched his sex. "One hand or two?"

Austin was careful. "I mean you can help him get in you because he's shy."

"He? Did you give him a name?"

"Long ago when I was about twelve."

"What did you name him?"

"Godzilla."

She burst out laughing and watched him to share the humor. "That was the great Japanese creature that all the kids just loved?"

"Yes."

She tilted her head and mentioned, "It was before my time."

He sighed rather dramatically. He mentioned, "Dealing with youngsters has always been a problem." He squinched his face up and looked at her as he said, "Twenty-four years old and *three* husbands already?" And he could have bit his damned waggling tongue off at the root, he was so appalled that he'd mentioned the dead husbands at *this* time, for crying out loud!

"Hush." She was suddenly very serious and quite cooled.

He went to her carefully. He put his hands on her naked sides and said, "They were lucky to've found you in time."

She told him soberly, "They were very kind."

He immediately wanted to get her mind off them, so he asked vulnerably, "Am I?"

She really looked at him. "I believe you are special."

"Thank you."

But she went on. "You've had a great deal of experience."

He sighed as he deliberately changed the line of talk. "I got this place when I was only about nineteen. My grandfather died and—"

"I was talking about sexual knowledge."

"Teach me."

Now what was a woman to think with that earnest request? She told him, "I know good and well that you are not innocent with women."

"What women?"

"The ones you've escorted in these last five years. Don't tell me you're an innocent!"

"I've been...used. Now listen! There are females out there who are earnest users of men!"

She laughed.

He was serious. "Men don't go with women only for sex. They like the company. They like to share. They like to show women around so they can see what the world is like! Men look at different things altogether and—"

"Men like to look at naked women."

His eyes went down her naked body, without his knowing it, as he said, "Men go to baseball games and they play touch football, and they're good at golf. They do all sorts of things. They go to a place they can look—"

"Houses of ill repute."

He took a step backward as if the wind had hit

him. He lifted his hands and said a very earnest, "*No!* You shock me."

And she laughed. How could she not? He was so earnest and careful and his hands and eyes were completely uncontrolled. He had no discipline for his hands and eyes at all. He was just like every other man. But she needed a baby.

She said, "I want you to give me a baby."

"We will. Not right at first, but we'll have a baby, and you'll be glad we waited a while so that we can get acquainted—"

"That's what *they* said!" Her eyes were wide with alarm. She went on, "They said we had all the time in the world, and that I was still too young to take anything like that on, at that time!"

"Honey—"

"That's what *they* called me. And they said we had all the time we wanted. And they are *all* dead!"

She began to cry and sought her gown to put it on. Her eyesight was blurred by the tears.

He was smart. He took her and held her close to his naked body and his arms were around her tightly. He said, "I'm healthy." He said, "I can give you a child." He said, "Darling, don't cry. We have all the time in—"

She cried harder. It was in despair. She didn't have to explain anything. Austin knew exactly what was riding her.

He told her, "We'll have a baby right away. I promise. But you need to marry me first. Honey, don't cry. Please. You wreck me."

She leaned back to speak to him in her distress— and she saw the tears in *his* eyes. She moved her hands on him to comfort him as she said, "It's all right."

So, of course, he took her to his bed. She wanted him, she needed him and she would have him yet again. He lay her on the bed and lay beside her as he smoothed back her hair.

He'd smoothed back her *hair!* Good gravy. She wanted him to make love to her! She moved her chest and wrapped one leg around him and made eager sounds. She thought that would trigger him. But he was so concerned for her that he held her and ignored Godzilla's anxiety.

The only way Iris got *her* way, was that she simply rolled Austin over flat on the bed, and she climbed up over him and guided him into her.

Austin was shocked. He gasped. He smiled. He licked his lips. He put his hands on her hips and held her steady and allowed her to make love to him…*his* way.

Men are really very sly and crafty.

But he saw to it that *she* was pleased and fulfilled. So was he. He allowed her to collapse on top of him and lie silent.

After a time, he said, "You greedy woman."

She said, "You shock me."

He said, "Are you going to do it all again?" And his voice trembled, but it was with hilarity.

Then he said, "You're mine. I've gotten an ankle bracelet with my name on it and I'm going to put it on your left ankle and brand you as mine. No other man can lure you."

Tears leaked slowly from her closed eyes. Her second husband had done that. She said nothing. She was silent. Then she told Austin, "I love you." And she'd come *that* close to adding, "too."

What would the three think of her lying now, replete, on yet another man? She had wanted to die and did her darnedest to achieve that. And yet here she was, lying on Austin's naked body.

She struggled from his arms and braced her hands on either side of him as she looked at Austin.

He smiled at her and wickedly said, "Not again!"

She told him seriously, "I love you."

"I know."

"I just wanted you to understand that I really do love *you*. It isn't the sex or the babies I want as much as I want you."

"As I want *you*." He was serious, watching her, caught by her earnestness.

"If we don't have babies...I would still want to stay with you. We could adopt some."

He nodded. He was watching her. She'd never talked this much with him, and he was serious. It was only then that he understood the depth of his love for her.

But he didn't immediately crush her against him in possession. He was smart enough to understand exactly how much he cared for her and how serious all this communication was for them.

He listened.

He moved his hands on her slowly as he listened.

He understood that she needed to clear the commitments between them and understand exactly what they wanted together.

Until this moment, their love had been superficial and exciting. Austin hadn't examined its depth. He was as committed as she. He had known that, but he hadn't really mentioned anything to her beyond sex and her being permanently with him.

He told her, "I love you from the bottom of my heart. If you couldn't have sex with me, I would still want you with me. Do you understand what I'm trying to tell you? This is very serious. I didn't know that until you tried to talk to me. Tell me this—do you love me enough? Or will you use me to have children?"

Great tears filled her eyes so that she was again

blind. She smiled so tenderly and she said, "I love *you*. I want *your* children."

So he asked carefully, "What about the kids you never had before...with them?"

"They didn't see any reason to hustle along and have kids. At that time, they weren't seeing into the future."

"Oh."

She explained, "They are gone. This is just about us."

"You've wanted kids all along the way. We'll start them on our honeymoon."

She considered. Then she said, "Six months after that."

He laughed. "I thought I'd have to do something rash tonight and get you pregnant here!"

"I couldn't figure you out—you were so delaying in the discussion of babies."

"I was afraid you might not realize that I love you. I'm concerned by how fragile you are, now, and I want you to get healthy before we talk about having kids."

She smiled rather wetly. She said, "So you don't mind if we do have babies?"

"I like kids. I love you. I want you healthy and sassy before we get you pregnant."

"That's not the first time you've mentioned my

being skinny!" Tilting her head several ways, she considered, "You want me fat."

"*Wellllll,* not entirely."

She laughed. Then her smile mostly left as she watched him and she asked, "You've thought about this all along?"

"I've wanted you forever. I could not believe *three* men were that quick. I'd thought you'd gone to school like a normal female. How was I to know some unknown would snatch you up that quick?"

"All three were very charming."

His voice a trifle rough with emotion, he said, "You miss them."

She could have said about anything and he would have accepted whatever it was, but she said softly, "They aren't you."

"I expected you to go to school and come back to me in four years. I'd never in this world thought some kid could lure you to him in that short of time."

"Yes."

His voice a trifle raspy from emotion, he asked The Question that had rattled him all along, "What was it that lured you to those three?"

She told him pensively, "They were so lonely and alone! They were so homesick. I felt sorry for them. They were so young."

"My God!"

Indignant, she retorted, "You'd not said even *one word* to me then!"

"You were an eighteen-year-old wet-nosed kid, for crying out loud! I was an adult!"

She looked down at him with a lifted nose and told him, "So was I—an adult. I was going to college in San Antonio."

"Well, hallelujah!"

"Don't be so snotty. It was an event for me. I needed the city shine."

He said with some hostility, "So you married three men."

"They were good friends."

His temper went up for the first time since then. "To you? How come you were such good friends with—"

With some surprise, she explained, "They were good friends among themselves and with their friends."

He lectured her just a tad late. "Then there was no need at all for you to've married them and smoothed out their lives!"

She was indignant. "That sounds very snotty of you."

"I was appalled!"

"Why would you be appalled when I married the first two? I can see your shock with the third—"

"I'm surprised you noticed, by then, that you'd had three husbands."

She sat up and looked down at him. She said, "Well, if you're *that* surprised, then I'll just go on home and—"

He looked at the ceiling and moved out his hands as he said, "Good God, help me with this strange and…careless woman!"

In a snit she widened her eyes and said through her teeth, "I'm a lady."

"This lady." That was not very easily done and it was obvious that he was not only reluctant, he was mad. Well, angry.

She lifted her chin as she inquired, "If I'm not a lady, then what am I? A…harlot?"

He snarled, "A *child* who has been stumbling blind!"

Of all things, she laughed. She laughed out loud and then she put her hand over her mouth and her eyes danced with humor.

How annoying.

He slid his eyes over at her a couple of times. Then he had trouble controlling his own humor. He sighed a couple of giant sighs, and he was annoyed that she had broken up the quarrel so easily. He'd been furious at her ever since she was eighteen and married that first husband!

How was a man, who was supposed to be an

adult and in control, to tackle a female who'd had *three* husbands and was still only twenty-four? He was five whole years older than she, and he had no way to control her, at all.

She was as she was. And she'd sure as hell not change. He looked at her, and he saw the humor dancing in her eyes.

So *that* was why those three had married her! No wonder. All they needed was to share that humor. That and her body.

Austin looked down her as men do and he saw how skinny she was, but remembered that she had been even skinnier. A woman who had suffered. How could he be so selfish? He'd wanted her all his life since he was sixteen and saw her at the age of eleven.

She'd worried about animals, her sisters, her little brother—and him.

He was five years older than she. He was an adult and she was just barely getting there. He looked at her. He was vulnerable.

She'd watched him with those big eyes as he'd played ball and hockey and run himself ragged on the court playing basketball. She'd yelled and clapped and been involved. He'd thought she was too young, then.

She was still too young.

He sighed with great age and endurance.

She giggled.

He said crossly, "I'm in a bad mood, and you're not paying attention to me at *all*. Behave!"

She put her head back and just laughed, so softly and with such tolerance! How dare she?

He smiled. Damned if he hadn't done exactly that! A man ought to be in control! He sighed with great endurance and looked off to the side, then back at her, his eyes drawn to her like metal to a magnet.

Ten

It was 2:00 a.m. when Iris put her key in the door and slid quietly into the house.

In the dark, wearing her nightgown and a wrapper, her mother got up from a chair and just about shocked Iris out of her shoes. Well, she was carrying the shoes to be silent. She exclaimed to her mother, "What are you doing up at this hour?"

"I've been debating if I should have the police find your dead body."

Iris laughed quietly.

Her mother inquired, "He take the tin top off his car with steel snip scissors?"

"The windows were open."

"So?"

"We're going to be married next month."

"Not until then?"

Again, Iris grinned as her mother hugged her. She said to the older woman, "How can I thank you for all you've done for me?"

"You've done it all. You're alive."

Softly, Iris mentioned, "It's been odd."

Her mother nodded gently. "I would imagine."

Iris looked out of the window at the night as she commented, "I can't believe Austin is still available."

Her mother agreed. "That is strange."

"When the time is right, I'll ask him how come he decided to be a single man."

Her mother inquired, "And if he tells you he was waiting for you?"

Iris shrugged and suggested, "Or if he tells me other women are crowding him outrageously and this is escape?"

Edwina's eyes were already teary. She smiled as she said, "Get some sleep."

"How come you're waiting up this late for a three-times married woman?"

"I love you."

"Ah, Mom. What would I have done without you?"

Edwina said softly, "You'd have survived. You're really very strong."

Remembering the time she was silent and just about comatose, Iris replied, "Yeah. I noticed."

Her mother understood Iris exactly, and she said, "You were in a time of grief. You came out of it. It was time."

"Do you really believe that?"

Edwina repeated softly, "You'd either help yourself to recover, or you'd have died. You had us all concerned for you."

Iris looked out the window into the silent night. "And I was so involved with myself that I didn't even notice you all and how kind you've been to me."

"We were here. You did know that. We backed you."

"Yes."

"But it was Austin who brought you out of your grief. He is a man."

"He is." She smiled. "He is so funny."

"Sometime tell me about it. I must go to bed. Sleep well, child."

Iris smiled. "I'm now a woman."

"Congratulations."

"It's taken a while. Good night, Mom. You are a gem. Daddy's lucky to have you."

Her mother replied softly, "So am I lucky, with him."

They hugged gently and separated.

Since the house was so big, Iris went to her room quite easily, without waking anyone.

Since she had her own shower, she quietly rinsed off, and she smiled the whole, entire time.

In pajamas, Iris slid into bed and covered herself. She sighed. She smiled. She turned over and slept. She dreamed.

Everything went...her way. That was how dreams should be made.

Over in his home, Austin paced and breathed. He appeared to look around, but he wasn't at all lucid. He just thought of Iris.

How come she wouldn't spend the entire night in his bed with him? She was always in a hurry to get home so that her mother could go to bed. Mrs. Smith was a stickler. He considered her. She'd make a good grandmother for their kids.

And Austin remembered when Iris had married each of those damned budding men and was kept away from him! It had shocked him. She'd appalled him! How was a man to control a female? He'd do it. Now *he* had her.

Well, not yet, but soon.

And he groaned at the length of time before he

could have her *all* the time…close. He finally went to bed because it was so late, and he went to sleep because he'd been so…thoroughly loved. He knew that. He smiled with his eyes already closed and he actually did go to sleep.

So it was the next evening that Austin went to Iris's house, slicked up and tidy. He smiled the whole entire time and didn't say much.

Iris came down the stairs looking just gorgeous and she exclaimed, "How nice to see you!" as if she hadn't expected him to visit.

"I've gotta talk to your daddy."

"Oh?" She moved her body and lifted her head and tried not to smile too much as she asked, "One of our cows got out?"

"No." He watched her and his eyes were just a twinkle of delight. "I'm gonna see if he'll allow me one of his daughters for a wife."

"Oh?" She said that yet again as she looked around. "Any of *my* sisters?"

And watching her with eyes that twinkled, he told her, "You."

She pretended astonishment and put her hand on her chest as she gasped, "Me? Uh…I?"

He was tolerant. "Yep, you're the oldest and they've been trying to get rid of you, more than—"

She gasped in shock but she mostly laughed.

* * *

So Austin was given the private meeting with Mr. Smith. Iris's daddy had a very tough time giving his agreement. Iris was so fragile.

Only Austin knew how wickedly romping she could be. He didn't mention that, he just told Mr. Smith that he knew exactly how to care for her and that she'd be all right with him.

So her daddy gave Iris in a fourth agreement to yet another man who would be the husband to his eldest daughter. She was twenty-four. This would be her *fourth* husband? It boggled Mr. Smith. He made no comment. He shook Austin's hand and just wondered if Austin would survive…her.

Among all those who lived in the area, no one was shocked by the engagement. The whole, entire family just was impatient and said, "Yeah" when told that Iris was to marry Austin. It was hardly a surprise. They said, "Fine."

Iris laughed.

So the sisters said, "Big deal." And, "What is different with your marrying a fourth time with yet another man?"

Iris replied, "They've all been kind, but Austin is special."

"How…special?" her littlest sister who was sixteen and curious asked.

"I love him."

So the sisters traded questions and asked, "Did you love the others?"

Iris replied gently, "In different ways."

"Like what?"

Iris said the obvious. "Men are very different, one from another. You have to look at them and decide."

So one of the sisters had to comment, "You decided."

Iris smiled.

With the actual wedding preparations beginning, the sisters were amused and tolerant. They chattered and moved around and were...normal? Well, for them they were.

Their mother joined the girls as they all went to the attic. There, they went through all the old marriage gowns and discussed the actual age of those gowns, who'd worn them in all those years and who had left which husband. It was part of their family history.

Actually, the discussion of the ancestors was among her mother and three sisters. Iris was so bemused by her love that she didn't pay much *real* attention. She smiled and looked at them, but she thought about Austin.

They met now, at rather odd times, and held each

other. They smiled and smiled and smiled. Austin never did mention her other husbands—out loud— at that time. He just wanted her to be his wife.

But there were those people who thought a fourth husband, for a woman like Iris, was pushing the ring just a tad. He was patient.

So, the attic's precious, old, chosen gowns were carefully cleaned and pressed gently. The cleaners gasped and smiled and discussed and looked over the materials…and they were envious.

It was no wonder that everybody, all around the area, knew exactly what was going on. The telephones? The grocery? Who was the gossip who had spread the news? No one knew. Each person appeared to have been told by someone different. The coming marriage was just about instantly known. The sending of cards with invitations was a tad useless.

But all those dear people were so touched and pleased for Iris and her family that the time before the wedding was special.

The gatherings—insisted on by the various kin and friends—were exhausting.

Everybody went to *all* of the luncheons or bridge playing or evening dinners. It was a hassle and everyone was totally exhausted long before the wedding.

Iris gained probably five more pounds! Austin asked her, "You pregnant?"

She said, "Good gravy! How come you ask *that?*"

And he said, "You're less skinny!"

She laughed and her eyes sparkled and she watched him.

Softly, he told her, "You look wonderful."

He was a smart man.

The Day finally came. Everybody was hyper. Except for the two who were to be married. They were in La-La land and just looked at each other and smiled. It was probably the only marriage, in all of time, that there wasn't a quarrel.

It seemed that *everybody* in the whole, entire area was at the church for the wedding. People who generally just skipped the weekly church were all there for the wedding! How shocking for the pastor whose brain had to scramble in order to remember the absentee names.

Probably the most interesting guest was Charles Bing who was the retrieved, escaped felon. It was he who'd left the company of the other escapees and returned to Austin's house...and gone back to the clink.

So had the others, but it had taken a while for the cops to capture them.

As a guest at the wedding, with an unexpected furlough, Charles Bing was handcuffed to a stocky, neatly dressed prison guard.

The time did come when the church organ became serious, and sentimental. Some of the ladies removed hankies from their purses or pockets to be prepared.

Their husbands sighed and did a single slow shake of their heads in tolerance. Women! How sentimental, the husbands would consider in tolerance—and then they would discreetly wipe an eye.

The minister came out and stood quietly as he smiled down the aisle. The town was so small that marriages weren't that often. He was delighted to be involved in one.

The bridesmaids and groomsmen came down the aisle with smiles. Iris's three sisters blushed and looked around at all the familiar people. However, those guests sitting in the church wondered what on earth those wicked usher friends of Austin's had said to those nice Smith girls to make them blush thataway! Even the seated men wondered, but it was avid curiosity not condemnation.

Then the bride came down the aisle on her father's arm, wearing the gown, which had belonged to her great-great-aunt. The gown was covered with pearls. Iris wouldn't sit down until she'd taken it off.

Her father was emotional. This was his daughter's *fourth* marriage. And he'd been a part of every one! How had all this happened? But he looked at her, smiling and blushing, as she mostly watched Austin who waited for her at the altar.

Austin grinned and blinked at tears and he saw no one else.

Her daddy stood behind her until the minister asked, "Who gives this woman—"

And her daddy stepped forward and said, "I do." Then he gave Iris's hand to Austin.

The marriage was the coupling of a lifetime—however, it was really just like all the other weddings. It was the emotion that spread and covered them all, which made them seem to be so different.

Iris cried all the way through the marriage. It wasn't just this marriage that caused her emotion; she was remembering all her other marriages and those precious men who were no longer on this earth.

But Austin was here. He'd triumphed. She was *his!*

With tear-filled eyes, Iris smiled at him as she gave her vows. She was so sweet that she just about unmanned Austin in one way, but she caught his heart entirely and he knew he would cherish her all the rest of his life.

An odd thing for a fourth husband to think.

But when the minister said they were to seal their vows with a kiss, they were already turned to each other and just looked so earnestly at each other with such love.

There wasn't a dry eye in the entire church!

The organ swelled, rattling the windows, and the new couple grinned at the minister and nodded, then they turned and allowed themselves to look first at their families on each side. Their families looked like precious people, and were. But the new couple also looked at all those people packed in attendance. They smiled. And all those in that small church just smiled right back in teary emotion.

She was now Iris Smith Osburn Dallas Alden *Farrell!*

Smiling at the happy, wet-eyed guests, the two walked from the chapel and stood in the room outside. They were surrounded and greeted by all the people as they left the church. They and the guests would all meet again at the Smith house. But as they stood there, Iris yawned.

That boggled, then alarmed Austin. She'd yawned? On her wedding day? And he became a tad indignant! As he watched, she stood next to him and her eyelids drooped closed!

He took her into his arms and held her in appalled fear. She was going back into that long rejection of life? Couldn't she tolerate him? She'd won him, and now she was going to reject him? Her fourth husband? He was just another man to her? Austin was sundered. He was stunned!

His head was down so that he could really look at her and hear her breathe. His arms were holding her. He was appalled. He bent his head with great emotion and asked, "Honey—?"

And she said to him softly, "I was up the whole, entire night fiddling with this damned dress! It would *not* hang on me as it should. I am exhausted! You'll probably just have to take me while I snore."

He laughed softly and squeezed the little hand he'd been holding in his own hot hand. His voice wobbled, "I'll fix it for you."

She opened her eyes and said, "*Now?* Who cares? The wedding is over!"

"Well...partway."

And she said, "That again."

A while later, they stood around and smiled and allowed people to shake their hands and they had punch. They did this at the church because there wasn't the room at home. The house was big, but there weren't enough of the family to keep people from exploring.

So the Smiths and some of their good friends waited and allowed the guests to drink the fruit juice, eat the dainty round yummies and chat and hug and comment.

One of those was Charles Bing who was hand-cuffed to a very uncomfortable, silent guard. Actually, the guard had begun to talk! He told the newlyweds, "Good luck!" That was all, but it was communication.

Then Iris thought about her own friends who would come over to spend the night—and they talked until midnight without any let up at all! What was different?

So she listened. She smiled. She nodded. And the ladies became very emotional and hugged her.

It was another one of God's gentle communications? How incredible that she was now old enough to understand. She looked for her darling husband. And he had moved so that he faced her and could watch her. He smiled at her.

And she got teary-eyed. How could she have survived? Had her Guardian Angel just pulled her skinny body off her bed and made her go with Austin that first time?

Tears came so easily, and this time it was only one that slid down her cheek, which was puffed with her smile.

Austin came over to her and leaned his head down a little so that he could softly ask very seriously, "You okay?"

"I love you."

His eyes became a little watery. He told her, "It's just a good thing you do. You're trapped with me for the rest of your entire life—and on beyond."

She looked up at him and just leaned her body on his for him to hold her. She watched his eyes and smiled as she said, "Okay."

That just about ruined him. He smiled at her, but his eyes were wet. He said, "I love you."

"I know."

"Tell me that I'm at least up there with those other three."

Very seriously, Iris told Austin, "You're way ahead of them. They were charming young men. I did love them, but it isn't the way I love you. You have to take good care of yourself and stay with me." She watched him closely, and her eyes were wet with tears.

Eventually, most of the crowd did leave the church's meeting place and went on home. However, the newlyweds did have a group who did not leave but followed the Smiths on back to their house.

There was food and conversation and hilarity and nobody went home until so late that they were all sleepy.

Naturally, the newlyweds finally went to Austin's house on his farm. The guests followed and didn't go inside, but they stayed out and sang and yelled and hit tubs with sticks.

Austin gave Iris cotton to put in her ears. He didn't turn on any lights. They stripped and showered together. He held her gently. She was exhausted.

She lay her head on his chest and said, "Tell me when I need to lift my leg to get out of the tub!"

He laughed softly.

But she heard it even through all the bangings and yellings and honkings.

She asked, "Do they do this *every* time there's a wedding?"

"No. They're just glad we finally made it. Have I mentioned that I love you?"

She smiled. "You got me."

"I can't believe this. It's what I've wanted for so long. I never thought it would actually happen."

"It's happened."

They kissed and they explored and they loved. All to the singing and yelling and battering of tubs outside. By then, the newlyweds really didn't notice all that noise. Of course, it *did* help that they'd put the cotton in their ears.

As they lay in bed, smiling, naked, replete, they gradually understood that their tub batterers had left!

They laughed. They took the cotton out of their

ears and they listened. And they smiled at each other. He told her, ''We're alone.''

''Finally.''

''Are you all right?'' he asked gently.

She tilted her head and said, ''Let's do it again.''

He collapsed and pretended to have passed out entirely.

She laughed in her throat. She asked, ''What are we to do?''

He suggested, ''Hush and go to sleep.''

She laughed softly.

He kissed her. He pulled her over on top of him and held her naked body against his. He ran his hands down her and sighed. ''I can't believe this is really true.''

''It is.''

''Finally...''

* * * * *

If you enjoyed what you just read,
then we've got an offer you can't resist!

Take 2 bestselling love stories FREE!

Plus get a FREE surprise gift!

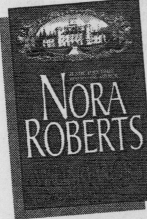

Based on the bestselling miniseries

A FORTUNE'S CHILDREN *Wedding:*
THE HOODWINKED BRIDE

by BARBARA BOSWELL

This March, the Fortune family discovers a twenty-six-year-old secret—beautiful Angelica Carroll *Fortune!* Kate Fortune hires Flynt Corrigan to protect the newest Fortune, and this jaded investigator soon finds this his most tantalizing—and tormenting—assignment to date....

Barbara Boswell's single title is just one of the captivating romances in Silhouette's exciting new miniseries, **Fortune's Children: The Brides,** featuring six special women who perpetuate a family legacy that is greater than mere riches!

Look for *The Honor Bound Groom,* by Jennifer Greene, when **Fortune's Children: The Brides** launches in Silhouette Desire in January 1999!

Available at your favorite retail outlet.

SILHOUETTE® *Desire®*

COMING NEXT MONTH

#1207 BLAYLOCK'S BRIDE—Cait London
The Blaylocks/Man of the Month 10th Anniversary

The minute Roman Blaylock came face-to-face with Kallista Bellamy, he knew she was the only woman for him. But the tempestuous beauty thought Roman was the man to blame for her misfortune—and she wanted revenge. Yet when she looked into his eyes, she realized falling for the enemy would be far too easy to do....

#1208 THE SECRETARY AND THE MILLIONAIRE—Leanne Banks
Fortune's Children: The Brides

When handsome Jack Fortune discovered he had a little girl, he turned to his faithful secretary, Amanda Corbain, for some badly needed baby-care lessons. But playing house with the delectable Amanda soon had Jack desiring to teach *her* some lessons...in love!

#1209 HIS WOMAN, HIS CHILD—Beverly Barton
3 Babies for 3 Brothers

He was the man she'd always loved, and now fate had made Hank Bishop the father of Susan Redman's unborn child. And soon after she opened her home to him, Susan dreamed of forever with the sexy loner who'd sworn he'd never fall in love....

#1210 SHEIKH'S RANSOM—Alexandra Sellers
Sons of the Desert

His country's heirloom jewel was stolen, and Prince Karim vowed to recover it—by kidnapping socialite Caroline Langley. But he didn't expect the primitive stirrings that she aroused. Now what would become of her if the prince's ransom was met...or if it wasn't...?

#1211 COLONEL DADDY—Maureen Child
The Bachelor Battalion

For three years Major Kate Jennings had secretly hoped that Colonel Tom Candello would ask her to marry him. Now that she was pregnant, he finally popped the question. But how could Kate agree to an in-name-only union when all she ever wanted was a happily-ever-after with Tom?

#1212 LET'S HAVE A BABY!—Christy Lockhart
Bachelors and Babies

When Jessie Stephens asked Kurt Majors for a clinical contribution to help her make a baby, he did the gentlemanly thing—he kidnapped her! And on his ranch, he set out to teach Jessie the joys of conceiving a baby the old-fashioned way....